D1540293

ENTICED

A Dangerous Connection

Melody Carlson

TH1NK, an
Imprint of
NavPress

NAVPRESS

Discipleship Inside Out®

NavPress is the publishing ministry of The Navigators, an international Christian organization and leader in personal spiritual development. NavPress is committed to helping people grow spiritually and enjoy lives of meaning and hope through personal and group resources that are biblically rooted, culturally relevant, and highly practical.

For a free catalog go to www.NavPress.com
or call 1.800.366.7788 in the United States or 1.800.839.4769 in Canada.

NAVPRESS, the NAVPRESS logo, TH1NK, and the TH1NK logo are registered trademarks of NavPress. Absence of ® in connection with marks of NavPress or other parties does not indicate an absence of registration of those marks.

ISBN-13: 978-1-60006-953-6

Cover photo by Shutterstock Images LLC, Supri Suharjoto

Published in association with the literary agency of Sara A. Fortenberry

Some of the anecdotal illustrations in this book are true to life and are included with the permission of the persons involved. All other illustrations are composites of real situations, and any resemblance to people living or dead is coincidental.

All Scripture quotations in this publication are taken from the *Holy Bible, New International Version*® (NIV®). Copyright © 1973, 1978, 1984, 2011 by Biblica. Used by permission of Zondervan. All rights reserved.

Carlson, Melody.
   Enticed : a dangerous connection / Melody Carlson.
      pages cm. — (Secrets; [bk. 6])
   "Th1nk."
   Summary: Praying for her own rags-to-riches story, impoverished sixteen-year-old Simi Fremont goes online to launch a modeling career but is soon caught in a dangerous web of slavery and human trafficking.
   ISBN 978-1-60006-953-6 (pbk.)
   [1. Models (Persons) — Fiction. 2. Human trafficking — Fiction. 3. Slavery — Fiction.
   4. Christian life — Fiction.] I. Title.
   PZ7.C216637Ent 2013
   [Fic]--dc23

                               2012046584

Printed in the United States of America

1 2 3 4 5 6 7 8 / 17 16 15 14 13

ENTICED

I wasn't always pretty. And a lot of the time I don't think I'm the least bit good-looking. That's because I still see myself as a too-tall, geeky misfit with an ugly unibrow and wild black hair. But then my appearance has changed this summer—dramatically. Having my mom's friend Trista work over my eyebrows did wonders, but I also found the right products for my hair. Consequently I've noticed that people look at me differently, and I even get random compliments.

Not from my peers, of course. Other than my best friend, Michelle, it seems like girls from school would rather sneer at me or make fun of my secondhand clothes. But occasionally an adult will make a nice comment.

Like yesterday when an elderly neighbor stopped me in the stairwell as I was going up to our apartment. "Well, look at you, Simi." Mrs. Norbert adjusted her glasses as she stared me up and down. "Why, you have grown into a beautiful young woman."

"Thanks!" I smiled brightly as I wrapped my beach towel a bit more snugly over my damp swimsuit. I'd just taken a cool-off dip in the apartment complex's tiny swimming pool.

"How old are you now?" She switched her shopping bag to the other hand, still studying me.

"I just turned sixteen last month," I said proudly.

"Is that all?" She pulled a set of keys from her pocket. "I thought you were older."

"Maybe because I'm tall."

Still eyeing me, she nodded with a thoughtful expression. "You know . . . you could probably take up modeling, if you had any interest in that sort of thing. You've got the right height for runway modeling."

I laughed, remembering the models I've watched on reality shows. "It sounds fun, but I doubt I'd be any good at it. I'm pretty much a klutz."

"But you can learn these things. You can learn to be grace-ful. Did you know I was a model when I was just a little older than you?" She stood straighter now, smoothing out her shoulder-length silver hair. "Of course, that was back in the sixties, but if I do say so myself, I was *something.*" She chuckled. "When I think back to those days . . . oh my . . . what fun I had."

Suddenly I saw this old woman in a whole new light. "Really? You were a professional model?"

She sighed with a faraway look. "Oh yes. I still have my portfolio."

"What's in a portfolio?"

"Mostly just photographs," she explained as she trudged up the next flight of stairs.

Keeping pace with her slow steps, I started to pepper her with questions. And she told me about how models would carry things called "tear sheets" as well as some black-and-white photos. She paused on the third floor, where we both live. "The portfolio would include a résumé as well as head shots and hand shots and even foot shots. Of course, there were also swimsuit shots and fashion shots. They needed to see the photos to decide if a model was right for a particular photo shoot." Mrs. Norbert walked down the corridor to her apartment and I stayed with her. "We girls would deliver these things to the ad agency or freelance photographer, and if we were lucky, we'd get a call-back, which meant we'd probably gotten the job." She smiled. "It was really quite exciting."

"Is that how models get work these days?" I was still standing by her door, which is four doors down from the apartment Mom and I share. "And do they get paid very much? And do you really think I could learn to do something like that? And get paid for it too?"

"You're just full of questions, aren't you?" She laughed as she turned the key in the lock and opened her door. "Well, maybe you should come by and talk to me about this sometime." She went inside and set her shopping bag on a table by the door.

"Yes," I said eagerly, still standing outside her door like a stray dog that had followed her home. "I'd like that. Mom keeps telling me I need to find some other ways to make my own money. And I've been doing some babysitting, mostly on the weekends, but modeling sounds a lot more interesting."

"Oh yes." She nodded. "It most certainly is. And I suspect it's much more lucrative than babysitting."

I glanced down at my damp towel and flip-flops. "I don't suppose *now* is a good time to talk."

She looked amused. "No, I don't think so, Simi. I'm beat after a long day at Marley's."

"That's right. You work at that women's clothing store, don't you?" I was careful not to say "that *old* women's clothing store," which is what most people my age call Marley's Dress Shop.

"I *manage* Marley's." She kicked off her shoes. "And it's not easy being on my feet all day, especially at my age." She pointed at me. "But besides the fact that I'm bushed, you are not dressed appropriately, my dear. Not if we're going to talk about fashion."

"Yeah. I know."

"Wednesday is my day off. Maybe you could stop by tomorrow. I do laundry and housekeeping in the morning. But if you came over, say around three, I might be able to tell you a bit about the modeling industry. At least I can tell you about what it used to be like, and I can show you my old portfolio, if I can find it. I suspect that some things don't change all that much."

"Thank you, Mrs. Norbert! I would absolutely love to do that. Thank you!"

"I'll see you at three then."

It's for that reason that I'm dressing very carefully today. Which is a challenge since my wardrobe is mostly limited to thrift-store bargains. But I want Mrs. Norbert to take me seriously. I want her to know I'm completely sincere about wanting a career in modeling. Because who knows? She might still have some connections in the modeling industry. Maybe this is going to turn into one of those life-changing moments.

I've read plenty of Cinderella stories. I love the movies about girls who go from rags to riches. I've always longed to be one of the lucky ones—I dream of getting discovered by Hollywood or winning *American Idol* or the lottery or simply marrying a rich, handsome prince from some foreign country. Why shouldn't I dream? And why shouldn't I want to escape my impoverished little ho-hum life?

I've even prayed to God, asking him to help me become something special so I can help my mom. As it is, we barely scrape by most of the time. Mom works hard as a receptionist at an escrow company where everyone takes her for granted. She tries to act like we're fine, like we're going to make it, but I'm not stupid. I know money is tight and if she lost her job, we'd be homeless. It doesn't help that my deadbeat dad, who abandoned us when I was five, can't be depended on for anything — including child support.

The way I see it, we're not much different from widows and orphans, and according to the Bible, God really cares for struggling people like us. So surely he must want to bless us. For that reason it doesn't seem wrong to ask God for a career as a supermodel. So as I try on the third outfit, I am praying hard for that to happen. Why not?

To my relief, after my mom got home from work last night, she was surprisingly supportive of my modeling idea when I explained my new plan to her. I was all prepared for some huge resistance. Instead, she was pretty positive.

"That's really generous of Mrs. Norbert," she said as we shared take-out Chinese food at our kitchen table. "Although I never would've guessed the old girl was a model. Go figure, huh?"

"Well, it was a long time ago. Like back in the sixties. Anyway, she told me to come by at three tomorrow. I'm going to dress really nice, kind of like it's an interview, you know? And maybe she'll believe in me enough to want to help me find some real modeling jobs."

Mom reached for the carton of spareribs. "At the very least, it should be good practice for you. I mean, for you to treat this meeting like an interview. But don't get your hopes too high, Simi. Even though it's kind of Mrs. Norbert to help you, her experience in modeling was a long, long time ago." She laughed.

"I know Mrs. Norbert's a little old." I felt slightly defensive of our elderly neighbor now. "But she seems to understand fashion — and she seems to believe in me."

Mom gave me a tired smile. "Well, I must agree with Mrs. Norbert that you're a pretty girl. Pretty enough to be a model. Of course, I'm biased. But you're certainly tall enough at five foot ten. And I know they like tall girls to show off clothes. Especially on the runway."

I frowned down at the egg roll in my hand. "But I'm not exactly skinny. I wonder if I'll have to lose weight. Maybe I should go on a diet right now." I set the egg roll back down.

"Lose weight?" Mom frowned. "Don't be ridiculous, Simi. You do not need to diet. Anyone who tells you that is perfectly crazy."

"But models are always stick thin. I have these curves."

"You have very nice curves." She firmly shook her head. "Don't even go there, young lady."

I shrugged and picked up the piece of egg roll again, then popped it in my mouth. Hopefully Mom was right. Although I don't think she's ever watched any of the reality modeling shows. Most of those girls seem very, very thin. And if they're not, they get kicked off.

"It would be nice if you could start earning money for college," Mom said wistfully. "Although I'm sure it's not easy to break into modeling. And it's probably really hard work, too."

"I'm willing to work hard. And I don't think modeling could be any harder than babysitting the Burk twins."

Mom laughed. "Well, don't give up your babysitting just yet, sweetie."

I cringe to think of the bratty two-and-a-half-year-olds I watch during the weekends. Leo and Lacy are more than just a handful; they are spoiled rotten. But their mom, Trista, is my mom's best friend, and I've committed to watching the twins on the weekends for the entire summer since their day care is only open on weekdays. But I learned early on that babysitting these two is no easy feat. Modeling would have to be easier.

As I try on my fifth outfit, I'm imagining informing Trista that she'll have to find someone else to watch her two adorable rug rats because I have found work modeling. What a day that will be! I finally decide on a pair of dark-gray skinny jeans, a silky sleeveless black top I sneaked from Mom's closet, and a pair of red high-heeled shoes I got for $5.99 at Payless last winter but never wore. The shoes make me more than six feet tall, which would normally make me feel ridiculously gigantic. But today I am imagining myself strutting down the runway with other tall models. I can see myself in designer originals as I move gracefully in the spotlight with all eyes on me. I can hear their applause and feel their admiration. It is fabulous!

As I work on my long dark hair and apply some makeup, trying to make everything look as perfect as possible, I imagine my smiling face on the cover of a slick glossy fashion magazine. Naturally, the photographer would airbrush the zit that's threatening to erupt on my chin right now. But for now I conceal it with my CoverGirl makeup and hope Mrs. Norbert won't notice the raised bump.

I'm just finishing up when my phone chimes and, of course, it's Michelle. "Are you all ready for your big appointment?" she asks. I can hear the slightly sarcastic edge to her voice, but that's Michelle. Even though she's fiercely loyal to me, she is skeptical about almost everything.

"I think so." I describe my outfit, and she insists I should send a photo to her.

"Just in case you missed something."

So I hold my phone out and, striking a pose, I take a shot and send it.

"I think that top is all wrong," she tells me after she's had a chance to check it out. "Makes you look too old."

"I don't think that matters. Mrs. Norbert thought I was older than sixteen and it seemed like that was a good thing."

"I guess that's up to you. If you want to look like that . . ."

I scrutinize my image in the mirror. "Well, I like it. I'm not changing a thing."

"Do you honestly think Mrs. Norbert can help you find a *real* modeling job?" Her voice is dripping in doubt now. I can't tell if she's really this cynical or if she's simply jealous.

"She was a professional model. She might know people."

"But she's so old, Simi. I'll bet everyone she knows is retired or dead by now."

Once again, I defend Mrs. Norbert, but even as I do, I realize Michelle is probably right. "So are you saying you don't think I can do this? Are you trying to shoot down my dream even before I have a chance to get started?"

"No . . . I'm just being realistic. And because I'm your friend, I don't want to see you disappointed or hurt."

"But what if this works? What if I really do make the right connections and get hired and make money and eventually get famous? Would you even be happy for me?"

There's a long pause now, and I'm reminded that Michelle isn't exactly what I'd call model material. For starters, she's only five foot two. Besides that, she's addicted to fast food, which has taken its toll on her weight. But she does have a pretty face. And her long curly auburn hair is very nice. If Michelle gave up fast food and shed some pounds, she might even have a future in fashion. Not that I plan to mention this to her. I value her as my best friend too much to go there.

"Yeah, sure, I'd be happy for you," she finally says. "But if you become famous, you'd probably drop me as your friend."

"I would not. You know I'm not like that."

"Okay then, good luck with your big appointment with old Mrs. Norbert." She chuckles like she's still not taking me seriously. "Let me know how it goes. Okay?"

"Yeah." I look at the clock in the kitchen. "It's almost three. I should probably head that way. I don't want to be late."

After I hang up, I wonder at her question. Does she really think I'd dump her as a friend just because I got rich and famous? I think of the times we've watched each other's backs while the mean girls used us for target practice. Not just with words either — although the painful sting of insults lasts longer than bruises and scratches.

But Michelle has always been there for me, and there is no way I would abandon her just because I landed a cool modeling career. If anything, it would help us both to hold our heads higher next fall when school starts. Maybe we wouldn't get picked on so much. Just one more reason for God to make my dreams come true!

I feel nervous and excited as I walk the four doors down. And the clicking of my high heels echoes in the hallway, sounding almost like someone else's footsteps. Or maybe I am someone else. Or becoming someone else. I can only hope.

I'm nearly to Mrs. Norbert's door when my heel catches on a crack in the floor and I nearly fall flat on my face. Catching my balance against the rough stucco wall, I manage to get back on my feet. I take in a deep breath, steadying myself, and smooth out my hair.

I am still just me. Simi Fremont. A desperate sixteen-year-old hoping for her big lucky break.

CHAPTER 2

"Come in, come in," Mrs. Norbert gushes as she opens the door. She has on a pair of white capri pants and a pale pink shirt. "Why, don't you look pretty. And very sophisticated, too." She tilts her head to one side, studying me carefully. "I really do think you might have what it takes, Simi."

I'm sure I'm beaming at her as I enter her small living room, which is identical to our living room except it's furnished in some interesting retro pieces. "Wow, what a totally cool room. Are these things really old or just reproductions?"

She laughs. "I suppose they are really old. My late husband and I invested in good furniture when we were in our twenties, and I've just never been able to let go of them."

I run my hand over a long, vinyl-covered white couch. "It reminds me of something I'd see in an old Audrey Hepburn movie."

"You watch Audrey Hepburn movies?"

"Yeah. Mom and I both like her a lot. *Breakfast at Tiffany's* is my favorite old film."

"Audrey Hepburn was the queen of style." Mrs. Norbert smiles. "So not only do you look like a model, you think like one too. I like that." She waves to the couch. "Go ahead and sit down. Let's talk."

I make myself comfortable on the sleek couch, attempting to cross one leg over the other, but the couch is so low and I lift my knee so high that I almost knock myself in the chin as I do this.

Mrs. Norbert laughs as she sits in an interestingly shaped orange chair. "You do it like this." She takes one leg and tucks it behind the other in a surprisingly graceful movement that makes her body resemble a *Z*, which seems pretty good for an old lady. "Go ahead and try it," she says.

So, trying to imitate her, I make several attempts until I finally manage to get one leg tucked neatly behind the other, but then I'm about to slide off the edge of the couch.

"You need to balance yourself. Hold your head high, like this. Don't slump your shoulders."

It takes me several more tries, but I eventually figure it out.

"Very good." She nods. "You'll have to practice that at home. And now I want you to gracefully stand up and go over to the door. Then pretend like you're just entering the room and sit down all over again."

Feeling silly and wondering what this has to do with modeling, I follow her direction. But I'm only halfway to the couch when she stops me. "No, no, Simi. Not like that. You look just like a goose."

She slowly stands and comes over to join me by the door. "Walk like this." Now she sort of saunters across the room; somehow she's moving her shoulders and her hips in a way that looks kind of smooth and yet sort of weird at the same time. And then she sits on the couch, folding herself into that *Z* position, and smiles at me. "See?"

"I . . . uh . . . I think so." So again I attempt to mimic her, but after a few steps, she sends me back to the door to try again. After about twenty tries, she is marginally satisfied with my performance and allows me to remain on the couch.

"I realize that most young women do not understand how to present themselves in a composed and professional manner anymore. But I strongly feel that a girl, one who wants to be noticed in the modeling industry, would be wise to carry herself with dignity and grace. That alone will get you attention."

I want to point out that I haven't noticed any of the models on reality TV walking, acting, or sitting like this, but I don't want to insult her. Especially since she is trying so hard to help me.

She comes over to sit next to me, reaching for a large black folder thing sitting on the glass-topped coffee table. "*This* is my portfolio," she says with almost reverence, as if it's the family Bible that's been passed down from her ancestors. "And although you can see that it's dated, you will get the general idea of what makes for a good portfolio." She proceeds to flip through glossy black-and-white photos of a very young and gorgeous blonde in a variety of shots.

"Wow, you were really beautiful."

"Thank you." She holds her head high.

"How long did you model?"

"Only a few years. About three and a half to be exact. That's when I met Mr. Norbert. And after we got married, he insisted I give up modeling. And then, of course, we had Belinda a year later. And as they say, the rest is history."

"How did you know you wanted to be a model?"

She sighs, smoothing her silver hair away from her face. "It was my mother's idea. She enrolled me in a class where I was taught how to walk and sit and practice good posture — just like I'm showing you. Then my mother's photographer friend offered to take pictures of me. Before I knew it, I was getting jobs modeling for department stores and tearooms, and I even did some print modeling, too."

"Print? You mean like magazines?"

"Yes. Advertisements. Magazines, billboards, that sort of thing."

"It must've been so exciting," I say.

"Oh yes, it was."

"Did you make a lot of money?"

"It was certainly good money. Especially for a girl my age. And I met a lot of interesting people." She smiles. "And, oh my, it was fun."

"And you really think I could do it too?"

She shrugs. "You're pretty enough. And you're tall enough. I should think you'd have as good a chance as anyone."

"What else do I need to do?" I ask eagerly.

She purses her lips in a thoughtful expression. "First of all, I want you to practice, practice, practice everything I've taught you today. Then I think you should come down to the store. I've been talking to the owner about having a fashion show there some evening, a little event to rev up more business. I'd planned on using some of our customers as models and, of course, they are older than you, but I think it would be a good experience for you as well."

"Really?" I try to imagine this. "You want me to model clothes from Marley's?"

"It will give you something to put on your résumé. Job experience. Meanwhile, we'll have to figure a way to start putting together a portfolio for you." She frowns as she closes her own portfolio. "I suspect you won't be able to afford a professional photographer."

I grimace. "Probably not."

"Well, perhaps there are new ways to do these things." She sighs. "I know we live in a new computer age, although I don't even know how to use a computer, other than the cash register at work. The truth is, I barely know how to use my cellular phone. My late husband was much more adept at these things than I am. He could even take photographs with his phone."

"I know how to do that," I tell her. "In fact, my phone takes pretty good photos. Do you think I could use that to make my portfolio?"

"I don't know why not. If the photos are good quality."

"And I know how to load them onto a computer. And how to post them on social networks and all that."

She brightens. "Well, perhaps that is the way to make a portfolio nowadays."

"Yes," I say eagerly. "Most people communicate through e-mail and social media. I'll bet I can build an electronic portfolio."

She waves her hand. "Maybe you can. But all that technology is Greek to me."

Now I'm excited as I imagine putting on different outfits and taking various shots of myself as I build an electronic portfolio. "I'm sure I can do this," I tell her enthusiastically. "And maybe I can get Michelle to help me."

"That sounds like a good plan, Simi. And I'll find out when we can schedule the fashion show at Marley's. In the meantime, you work on your portfolio and do not forget to practice, practice, practice." She hands me her portfolio. "Why don't you take this with you, dear. It might help you to pose for your own photographs."

"Really?" I'm surprised she'd part with this treasure. "You don't mind if I borrow it?"

"Just take good care of it."

"I will." I nod.

She gets a thoughtful look now, as if she's making some sort of plan. "And I will try to contact someone from my old agency."

"Agency?"

"Modeling agency. Anyone who needs a model—whether it's for a fashion show or advertising or whatever—goes through an agent. They call your agent and explain what they're looking for. Then the agent decides which models are best suited for the assignment and sends them out. If you're chosen for the job, your agent goes over the contract for you, and some agencies, like the one I worked for, will pay you an advance." She makes a slightly smug smile. "I was with Ford."

"Ford, the cars?"

"No. Ford, the modeling agency. Just the most prestigious modeling agency in the country. Perhaps in the world. At least they were when I was working for them. Ford was started in New York by the Ford family, back in the forties I believe. But there's one in Los Angeles, too." She stands, rubbing her hands together eagerly. "In fact, I should give them a call *right now*. Perhaps Bernice still works there."

"Bernice?"

"Bernice McDaniels was a model with me in the sixties. But she became an agent after she was too old to model anymore. It's possible she's still working there now." She heads for the kitchen. "Excuse me while I try to see if I can find their number."

Feeling excited and hopeful, I wait, eavesdropping as Mrs. Norbert speaks to someone at this prestigious Ford agency. Is it possible that before I leave here today, she will have found a real connection for me? At what might be the biggest modeling agency in the world? I'm so excited I can barely breathe. But when she returns, I can tell by her expression that she hasn't been successful.

"Bernice has passed on," she tells me in a dejected tone. "More than five years ago." She shakes her head. "Lung cancer. Very, very sad."

"I'm sorry."

"Yes, so am I."

"And the woman I spoke to sounded very young. Naturally, she'd never heard of me before, but that was no excuse for her rudeness."

"She was rude to you?"

She waves her hand. "Well, dismissive anyway. She told me that their agency was not actively seeking new clients. In other words, she gave me the brush-off." She sighs. "Oh well. Ford is not the only fish in the sea. I suspect there are dozens of perfectly good agencies in the Los Angeles area."

"Yes, I'm sure there are."

"So, you go and work on your portfolio. And practice everything I showed you until it feels natural. And I'll let you know about the fashion show at Marley's."

"And what about agencies?" I ask eagerly. "Should I look into finding one that is interested in me?"

"Oh no, dear. Not yet. It's too early for that. There are things we should work on. And then we should do some research and find out what agency would be best for you. I'm sure I still have some friends around who can help us with these questions." She sadly shakes her head. "Oh, poor Bernice . . . and lung cancer. Well, it's no wonder since we all smoked far too much back then. But who knew?"

I express my sympathy again and, clutching Mrs. Norbert's old portfolio to my chest, thank her for her time, promise to practice, and then leave. I'm so excited about making my electronic portfolio that I can barely contain myself as I hurry back to our apartment.

I kick off the red high heels, which are killing my feet, then go straight to my bedroom, which is still a mess from all the outfits I tried on, and frantically dig through the pile of clothes. Somehow I need to put together some stylish-looking ensembles. There's no time to waste in getting my portfolio together. It's already the end of June, and if I'm going to make it as a model this summer, I need to get to work.

Finally, I've arranged what I think are some good outfits. I lay them out on my bed, complete with shoes, sandals, and boots, and I take turns trying them on. I even attempt to take some photos, but I realize that to get good quality shots, I will definitely need some help. So I call Michelle and enthusiastically tell her about my meeting with Mrs. Norbert and how she lent me her portfolio, and how I'm going to make my own electronic portfolio, and even that I'm going to model in a real fashion show. However, I don't admit that it's only at Marley's Dress Shop. After all, Michelle doesn't need to hear all the details.

Fortunately, she catches my enthusiasm, and before I hang up, I have her word that she'll come over here tomorrow to play photographer for me. Not only that, but she promises to bring along her mom's digital camera as well as some of her own accessories. Michelle might not like buying clothes so much, probably because of her weight, but she adores accessories and has a great selection of costume jewelry, scarves, hats, and belts. Just what I need to round out my outfits and look like a real fashionista.

While my mom vegges in front of the TV, I spend the evening cruising through agency websites, but remembering Mrs. Norbert's advice, I resist the temptation to start filling out applications. I want to wait and see if she comes up with something. Besides, I should have my portfolio ready to go first. However, I do list the most promising websites in my Favorites folder. I also create a new Facebook page.

While my other page, the one I started back in middle school, is mostly just a way to connect with a few people, primarily Michelle, sharing goofy photos and jokes and various links, this new Facebook page will be devoted entirely to fashion — and to me. I can't wait to start filling it up with my portfolio shots. I really feel like I am on my way, and maybe by July I'll start landing some real modeling jobs. It could happen — I believe it!

CHAPTER 3

Michelle shows up around ten on Thursday morning, lugging in two bags filled with her fabulous accessory collection. Together, we finesse my outfits, deciding what goes with what, and an hour later I am posing in front of the cream-colored sheet we'd taped to the wall that separates the kitchen from the living room. But after a few shots, Michelle decides that our lighting is insufficient. So we pull up all the blinds and then get every single lamp in the house. After arranging them on tables and stools all around me, we remove the lamp shades and turn the lights all on.

"Much better," Michelle says as she takes more photos.

Although the apartment looks like a hurricane hit it and the lamplight is making it uncomfortably warm, Michelle and I press on into the afternoon, taking more and more photos. I pose in dresses, pants, shorts, swimsuits, skirts, even my Hello Kitty pajamas and fluffy pink slippers, which look a little goofy, but as Michelle points out, you never know. Finally, we're both exhausted, and I have less than thirty minutes to put the apartment back into place before Mom comes home.

I turn on the AC, although I'm not supposed to do this since we're on a strict budget, but Mom will freak out over how hot it is in here. As I'm running around frantically restoring order, Michelle is loading all the photos onto my computer for me.

"Some of them are really good," she says as she returns to the living room. "You're actually pretty photogenic."

"Really?" I pause from adjusting the lamp shade. "You think so?"

She nods. "Maybe you really will make a good model."

"Thanks!" I hug her. "And thanks for your help today. No way could I have done this without you."

"So you won't forget me once you become rich and famous and get your photo on the cover of *Elle* or *Vogue*?" I can hear the teasing tone in her voice, but her expression is serious.

"You will always be my best friend."

"Cool." She starts collecting her accessories now, loading them into the bags. "I can't wait to see your portfolio when it's done."

"I'll send it to you," I promise. "My goal is to get it put together before this weekend. And then I plan to send it out right away."

"Are you still babysitting for the bratty Burk twins?"

"Yeah." I replace the lamp on the end table. "Don't remind me."

We've just finished up and Michelle is leaving as Mom gets home. Fortunately the apartment looks fairly normal now, and Mom is none the wiser about how I tore it all up. I can tell by her face that she's had a hard day at work, and feeling enthused from our photo session, I even offer to fix dinner.

"That would be fantastic." She dumps her purse on the table and kicks off her shoes. "And I'll take a shower and put my feet up."

As I scavenge in the freezer and the kitchen cabinets for

something interesting to make for dinner, I try to imagine what it would feel like to have some interesting food and ingredients at my fingertips for a change. Maybe someday. In the meantime, we'll have to settle for frozen chicken enchiladas, which I heat in the microwave. But I do slice up a cantaloupe to go with it, and Mom doesn't complain at my meager offering. I tell her a little about our photo shoot, but her enthusiasm has definitely gone downhill since yesterday.

Finally, she admits that she's worried the escrow company is thinking about letting people go. "I might have to start looking for another job," she says as we're finishing up dinner.

"Oh . . ." I frown as I clear the table. "Well, I'll do what I can to help out."

"And don't give up your babysitting job," she says as she gets up.

I promise her that I won't, and after she retreats to her room, I continue to clean the kitchen. It's only a matter of time until I'll be making enough money to not only quit babysitting but help out if Mom loses her job.

I really believe my life is about to change—doors are about to open. As I scrub the sink, I remember back in middle school when Hannah Whittier made fun of me for wearing a Gap shirt that she was certain had belonged to her. Naturally I denied it. But when she claimed her mom had donated a bunch of her old clothes to a nearby Goodwill, I'm sure my face gave me away—I had found the shirt there the previous weekend.

She and her mean, snooty friends thought that was hilarious. They called me Miss Goody Goodwill for the rest of the year. I never wore that shirt again, and I learned to shop at thrift stores in other towns.

As soon as I'm done in the kitchen, I go straight to my room and begin sorting through the photos Michelle took today. This laptop is pretty old and slow—Trista gave it to my mom several years ago when she upgraded to a better one—but I'm the one who uses it most of the time. And fortunately, the apartment building has free Internet. I'm so driven to get this portfolio right that I work until I'm so tired I can barely keep my eyes open. To my surprise, it's almost two in the morning when I finally shut down.

The next day I get up and go straight back to work on this project. After hearing about Mom's job situation, I am determined to get this thing up and running this weekend. I make a folder containing about forty photos similar to the shots in Mrs. Norbert's portfolio, all of which I've titled and numbered. And if I say so myself, it looks fairly professional. At least to me. In the afternoon, I load about twenty photos onto my Facebook page.

And then Trista calls to ask if I can babysit tonight. "I know it's short notice and I know you usually go to youth group on Fridays, but the UPS guy that always delivers to the salon, you know the one who's always so sweet and polite, well, he finally asked me out, and he seems like such a good guy and I just couldn't say no, Simi."

I want to tell her no and that I really need to go to youth group, but I remember Mom's job situation and reluctantly agree. Besides, the twins go to bed at seven thirty so I'll only be chasing after them for a couple of hours. So, really, it will be a piece of cake compared to the weekend. Besides that, I can take my laptop and continue to work on my project once they're asleep.

"So can you be here by five?" she asks hopefully. "To help with the twins while I get ready? You know what a handful they can be when they know I'm going somewhere in the evening."

"Yeah, I do know. And yeah, I'll be there by five."

So at a little before five, I leave Mom a note. And with the laptop in my backpack, I trudge down the stairs to Trista's apartment on the first floor. Trista and the twins have only lived here about a year. They moved in right after Trista's husband, Scott, turned into a three-time loser. At least that's what Mom and Trista call him now. First Scott lost his job, then he lost their house, and finally he lost Trista and the kids by having an affair with one of their neighbors. I used to think he was a pretty cool guy, but now I know he was just a big jerk, which seriously makes me question my discernment skills when it comes to men.

Not that I need to be too concerned about that just yet. But when I become a model, I might need to hone my ability to detect whether or not a guy is the real deal. I hope Trista is right about this UPS dude. She's been crushing on him for a couple of months now, and I must admit he seems like a good catch. And for Trista's sake, I hope he's all she thinks he is.

"Yay, you're here," she tells me as she opens the door with a flattening iron in her hair. "Leo, get off that table! Right now, before you fall and break your neck."

I hurry past her and scoop Leo off the edge of the coffee table, tickling him as I flop him onto the floor. Naturally, he thinks this is a great game and climbs right back on the table again. And before long, Lacy is attempting to do the same. To distract them, I go to their room where I act like I'm playing with their toys, and seconds later they show up and I manage to keep them entertained while Trista gets ready for her big date.

As she does her hair and makeup and gets dressed, she calls out to me, telling me all about Kent, the UPS guy, and how he was so shy when he asked her out and where they are meeting. "What do you think of this outfit?" she asks as she pops into the twins' room.

I study the short skirt and snug top and frown. "You want my honest opinion?" I ask tentatively.

She looks down. "Too much, huh?"

"Or too little."

She laughs. "I can't believe a teenager has more fashion sense than I do."

"Hey, you're great when it comes to hair and eyebrows. But since it's your first date . . . well, maybe you should hold back a little."

She nods. "You're absolutely right."

When she returns, she's dressed much more conservatively in a sleeveless turquoise blue dress. "Very classy," I tell her. "And it makes you look tan."

She holds up two pairs of shoes. "Which ones?"

I point to the sandals in the same color of blue, then I suggest she might want to put silver earrings with it. "Turquoise and silver look pretty together," I say, like I'm suddenly an expert. Then, since the twins are occupied with the block tower we were building, I follow her back to her room and briefly tell her about my modeling plans and how Michelle and I took all the photos for my portfolio yesterday.

"Wow, that's impressive," she says as she holds up a pair of silver hoops. She turns and looks closely at me. "With your height and those long legs, you probably would be a good model." She slips in a hoop. "You're pretty enough too."

I thank her and then, hearing a crash and squeals, I hurry back to the twins' room to see their tower has fallen and they are now pelting each other with the blocks. Trista leaves a little before six, just as I'm dishing out some macaroni and cheese with a few frozen peas tossed in and trying to get the brats situated in their booster chairs. It was so much easier when I could buckle them into the high chairs, but they outgrew those recently. I manage to entice them to eat most of their dinner with the promise of yogurt-cicles for dessert. And then I get them stripped down and into the bathtub around seven.

By the time they're in pajamas and wrestled into bed, I feel exhausted. Fortunately, they seem tired too. And after a picture book and bedtime prayer, they are drifting off. I just hope I don't drift off too because I still want to work on my portfolio and perhaps even fill out some modeling agency applications tonight.

Finally, convinced that they are really asleep, I tiptoe from their room and go straight for my computer, where I pull up my Favorites file and peruse through the modeling agency websites. I know Mrs. Norbert told me I wasn't ready yet and that she wanted to help me with this, but I also know she is old—and she doesn't move very fast. What if it takes her weeks to figure something out? Or what if she gets distracted and forgets? I really feel like I need to take matters into my own hands. Especially with Mom's situation at work. Besides, *I am ready.* Everyone usually tells me I'm old for my age. And I've managed to put together a pretty good portfolio. Even Michelle, the skeptic, seemed almost convinced that I could do this.

At first I think I'll apply only to the most-impressive agencies, and then I decide why not just go for it and apply to all of them? Well, except for the ones that are obviously schools looking for paying students, since I obviously can't afford that. I figure that filling out a lot of applications is kind of like buying a bunch of lottery tickets. It should improve my odds. The forms are all pretty similar, kind of like job applications, except they ask about things like height, weight, hair and eye color.

Finally, it's almost ten and I've filled out about twenty applications and can barely keep my eyes open. Remembering that models need their beauty sleep and that I had a late night last night, I call it quits and give in to the couch, where I quickly fall asleep.

When I wake up, it's almost eleven, but I don't expect Trista back until midnight. I'm about to close down my laptop when I notice that I've got an e-mail, so I decide to check it. To my stunned amazement, one of the modeling agencies has already responded to my application! Okay, it's not a very personal letter and is worded rather formally, which makes me think it's probably an automated response. But since they're inviting me to submit my portfolio to them, I happily comply.

Before long, the folder of my forty best photos is on its way to Top Models and Actors Inc., and I am feeling very hopeful. This is probably just the beginning. I'm sure I'll be hearing from even more of them by tomorrow. And even if this e-mail was an automated response, someone will receive my photos and, perhaps by Monday, I will hear back from them and, maybe by July, I will begin modeling and I can give up my babysitting job.

Of course, this reminds me I should probably check on the twins, although I'm sure they're still asleep. I tiptoe down the hall and peek into their room, where I can see by the light of the Winnie the Pooh night-light, they are both still sleeping soundly. I must admit that Leo and Lacy look awfully sweet and innocent and dear as they're snoozing peacefully. To my surprise, I feel unexpectedly protective of them. Maybe it's a maternal feeling. Anyway, I'm sure it will evaporate by tomorrow when I'm chasing them around this place.

Trista gets home a little after midnight, and I can tell she's had a good date. She promises to pay me next week, and I tell her I'll see her again in the morning. Then I hurry back up to our apartment and go to bed. But now I find it's hard to get to sleep because I am so jazzed. I am imagining myself as a client for Top Models and Actors Inc. I can see myself strutting down the runway. I feel the heat of the spotlight on me. I can hear the applause of people watching. And suddenly I'm thinking—why should I limit my dreams to only modeling?

Perhaps I can have a career in acting as well. I've always had an interest in drama and have had minor parts in several plays. Why shouldn't I be on the big screen as well as on the runway? Lots of models make this transition. Why not me?

Suddenly it feels like my future is stretching out before me like an inviting highway that's filled with promise and hope, and I can't wait to see where all this is taking me. Now if only I could go to sleep!

CHAPTER 4

The next day I sleep in and have to scramble to make it to Trista's by ten. Fortunately her salon is only a few minutes away, so she's only a few minutes late. But I did remember to grab my backpack, which still has my computer in it. And although I don't get a moment to check my e-mail until I've finally put the twins down for their afternoon nap, I'm excited to discover I've received a second message from Top Models and Actors Inc. I eagerly open it to find it's from someone named Marcia Phillips.

> *Dear Ms. Fremont:*
> *Thank you for sending your portfolio. I am pleased to tell you that we are impressed with your photos and want to consider adding you to our clientele list. Please let us know when we can schedule a conference call with you. We have a big event next week and I think you have just the look to be part of it.*
>
> *Sincerely,*
> *Marcia Phillips*
> *Vice President, Top Models and Actors Inc.*

I'm so excited I have to control myself from letting out a whoop as I do a silent happy dance all around the living room. Then I call Michelle and tell her the good news.

"Wow, that was fast. Don't you think that's a little suspicious?"

"Suspicious?"

"Well, you never know. There are a lot of creeps out there, Simi."

"These guys are totally legit. You should see the TMA website." Then I tell her how to find it, and after she goes there, she has to admit it's an attractive site and looks like a solid agency.

"Even so," she says, "you should do some research on them before you go sign yourself up for life."

"I'll hardly be signing up for life."

"Yeah, well, for all you know they could be making sleazy movies."

I laugh. "Did you see all the photos of their models? Did you read about all the things their clients have been featured in? These guys are the real deal, Michelle. It's all completely aboveboard."

"Well, people can lie, you know."

"Oh Michelle." I release an exasperated sigh. "You can be such a buzz kill sometimes."

"Sorry. Just call me a realist."

"Well, when I start bringing in the big bucks and become famous, I'll try not to say I told you so. *Okay?*" I laugh as I flick through the beautiful faces on the TMA website. I can't wait until I see my face up there with them. This is beyond exciting!

After a few more doubtful comments from Michelle, I make

an excuse to hang up, but really I just want to e-mail TMA back before the twins wake up. However, I'm trying to carefully word my e-mail. I want to sound smart and professional. And not overly eager. Not that I plan to play hard to get, but I want to make them really want me.

Dear Ms. Phillips:
Thank you for getting back to me so quickly. I am inter-
ested in talking to you. Because I'm working this weekend,
it might be best to schedule a call for next week. Monday
at the soonest—

I stop typing and study this. Maybe I should clarify that although I'm working, it's not a job I'm particularly committed to. I don't want them to think there's anything to keep me from working for them. So I go back and make some changes, explaining that I'm actually just babysitting for a friend. Then I give Marcia my cell phone number as well as our landline, saying I'll be available for a conference call anytime on Monday. *A confer-ence call!* I cannot believe it. I'm actually going to participate in a real conference call with a real modeling agency. This is beyond exciting.

My spirits are so buoyed by Marcia's e-mail that I'm filled with extra energy, and I'm actually eager to play with Leo and Lacy, keeping them happily entertained all afternoon. I even take them and their afternoon snack outside to the play yard, which means lifting them into swings and helping them onto the slide, basically a complete workout for me while they have all the fun. But I don't mind, because I'm almost certain that my babysitting days with them are numbered. As in number one—after Sunday, which I'm hoping will be my last day, I plan to give Trista my notice. Hopefully she'll find someone else without too much problem for next weekend.

When I go home, I tell Mom the good news and show her the website and she is very happy for me. "It was so wonderful of Mrs. Norbert to set you up like this." Mom points to the portfolio sitting on the coffee table. "Perhaps you should return that to her."

"Good idea," I say as I pick it up. "I'll take it to her now." I realize Mom's assuming that Mrs. Norbert found TMA for me and I should probably straighten her out, but right now I'm eager to tell Mrs. Norbert my good news. But when I knock on the door, it seems she's not home. I'm about to leave when I hear what sounds like someone crying out from inside the apartment.

"Mrs. Norbert?" I call out, wondering if I'm hearing things.

"Help me!" she cries out in a raspy voice.

"Mrs. Norbert! Are you okay?"

"Help!"

Now I try the door, which is naturally locked. "I'll be right back with Mr. Reeves," I yell. "Hold on!" Having no idea what is wrong with her, I shoot down the stairs, past Trista's, to the superintendent's apartment down on the end, where I pound on his door. "Mr. Reeves! Open up! Mrs. Norbert needs help."

I can tell I woke him up, but I quickly explain what's going on, and he grabs his keys and his phone and we both dash back up the stairs, where he opens the door and we find Mrs. Norbert on the floor. We both kneel to see what's wrong, and in a hoarse voice, she explains that she fell.

"I'm afraid . . . something is broken," she says breathlessly. "I can't get up. I couldn't get the phone."

Mr. Reeves is calling 911 now and I remain on the floor trying to soothe this poor old woman. "Do you want some water?"

"Yes, *please!*"

I bring back a glass of water and help her to sip it. Then I tell her that I brought her portfolio back. I'm tempted to tell her about the modeling agency, but she's in such pain that I don't think I should.

"I've been here for more than nine hours." She looks sadly up at the clock. "I thought I might just die here."

"I'm so glad I heard you."

"So am I. Can you call my daughter?"

"Yes, of course." I pull my cell phone out and she tells me the number and soon I'm talking to Belinda, explaining that her mother fell down and broke something. "An ambulance is coming," I explain. Mr. Reeves is still talking to the emergency people on the phone.

"Tell them to take her to St. John's and I'll meet her there," Belinda says.

Before long the paramedics arrive and I tell them what Belinda said. I hold Mrs. Norbert's hand as they check her out and load her on a gurney. "I'll pray for you. And I'll come visit you at the hospital," I promise. Then I watch as they wheel her down the hallway.

"What's going on?" Mom says as she emerges just in time to see the paramedics carrying Mrs. Norbert down the stairs.

I explain what happened and Mom hugs me. "I'm so glad you were there to help her, Simi. I'm sure she's grateful."

"I promised to visit her in the hospital."

"Well, let's give her time to settle in and get X-rays and whatnot. Maybe we can go in later this evening."

By the time we go to the hospital, Mrs. Norbert has been settled into a room, and thanks to some pain pills, she is resting peacefully.

"She broke her hip," Belinda explains. "But she was also having some heart irregularities, so they're keeping her overnight for observation."

"Poor Mrs. Norbert," I say.

"Yes. I'm afraid she'll have to give up her job at Marley's now." Belinda shakes her head. "And I'm bringing her home to live with me until she recovers."

"How long does that take?" I ask.

"The doctor said it could take months."

"Oh . . . I'll miss her."

"I figured this would happen someday," Belinda says. "I just didn't expect it so soon."

We visit awhile, but it's clear that Mrs. Norbert is not going to wake up anytime soon. I squeeze her cool hand and tell her I'll keep praying for a swift recovery, but when we leave, I figure it's going to be a while before she comes home. I'd really wanted to tell her about Top Models and Actors Inc., hoping to get some feedback from her. But now I'll have to figure this out myself.

Still, I'm sure she'd be happy for me. After all, she was the first one to believe in me — to encourage me that I have what it takes to become a model. Hopefully I will make her proud. Maybe I'll have launched a successful career even before she returns home to the apartments.

Mom and I go to early church on Sunday morning, and after that I go over to Trista's to babysit. Throughout the day I keep assuring myself that this might be my very last day to watch the twins and that I'll have a real modeling job within the week. That thought energizes me, and the twins and I have one of our best days ever.

In fact, by the time Trista comes home from the salon at four, I'm feeling like I was all wrong about these kids. They're not really brats. They're simply energetic. And if you play with them and enjoy them, they are actually rather sweet. In a way, I think I will miss them.

I almost tell Trista not to count on me next weekend, but then I decide to wait until after tomorrow's conference call. By now I know that Marcia Phillips and the head of the fashion department, a guy named Bryce Farrow, will be calling me at one in the afternoon. I cannot wait to speak to them. I'm praying I'll handle it right and not make a complete fool of myself.

On Monday I try to keep myself busy by completely cleaning my room and organizing my closet. I've never been so motivated before. But the idea of becoming successful and famous and rich is empowering. After I get my room into the best shape it's ever been in, I go to the computer and study my portfolio photos, as well as my Facebook page. I have accomplished so much in so little time and I can't help but think all my hard work is about to pay off.

It's a little past one when my fully charged cell phone chimes. Trying not to appear too eager, I answer it on the second ring.

"This is Marcia Phillips of Top Models and Actors," a female voice says. "Is this Ms. Fremont?"

"Yes, but you can call me Simi."

"Good. And that's such a pretty name. Perfect for a model. Simi, I'd like to introduce you to Bryce Farrow. He was very impressed with your photos."

"It's a pleasure to meet you," a deep voice says. "We're glad you contacted our agency. Have you contacted any other agencies yet?"

I admit that I filled out numerous applications. "But I haven't heard back from them yet."

"Well, that's typical," Marcia assures me. "We try to respond promptly when we feel an applicant has strong potential. That's how we manage to get some of the best models and actors."

"That's right," Bryce says. "We don't wait around."

"Well, I'm glad," I tell them. "I'm eager to start working."

"You are . . . that's wonderful," Marcia says. "So you're ready to give up your babysitting job?"

I laugh. "Yes, I think I can bear to part with that."

"I used to babysit too," Marcia tells me. "I can't say I ever missed it. How old are the kids you've been watching?"

"Two and a half," I say. "Twins."

She laughs. "Oh my. That would be a handful. Whatever made you agree to do that?"

"Well, Trista, their mom, is a friend of my mom's. And I kind of owed her a favor."

"You sound like a sweet girl," Marcia says. "Which brings me to a somewhat personal question. One we don't like to put on our applications, but because of the nature of the modeling job that's coming up, I must ask. If you don't mind."

"Not at all. What is it?"

"Well, because the campaign we're considering you for is for a rather conservative group, it's important for them to know that you are a *nice* girl. They will not hire anyone who has, shall we say, a bad reputation." She lets out a nervous laugh. "I hate having to ask this, but I've made the mistake of sending them some, well, unacceptable girls in the past and it's been very embarrassing for everyone."

"Yes," Bryce jumps in. "These people expect girls as pure as the driven snow, if you get my drift." He laughs. "No pun intended."

Although I'm a little surprised by these questions, I do

ENTICED · · · · [45]

understand what they mean, and as I consider it, I think it's reassuring that they are looking for "nice" girls. "Well, I've never been on a real date," I confess. "I've never had a boyfriend. If that's what you're talking about. And I made a purity pledge in my church when I was twelve."

"Perfect," Marcia tells me. "That's just what this campaign is looking for. Pretty girls who have lived a clean life. I'm so glad to hear you'll fit into this."

"That is a relief," Bryce says. "You have no idea what a rarity you are, Simi."

"So does that mean I got the job?" I ask anxiously. "I mean, will I become your client, part of your agency?"

"We still need to have a face-to-face interview," Bryce says. "And we'll want to take some of our own photos."

"Yes, of course," I say eagerly. "I know my photos weren't professional."

"Don't worry about that," Marcia says. "We'll take care of everything . . . that is, if we decide to sign with you."

Now I feel worried. What if they don't like me once they meet me in person? "So what's the next step?"

They explain that they'll need me to come to the studio. "Do you have transportation?" Bryce asks.

"Not really. But I can ride the bus or—"

"Or we could send a car for you," Marcia says. "Do you think we could arrange that, Bryce?"

"I don't see why not."

Soon it's decided that a car will come for me tomorrow morning at ten thirty. But now I feel a little uneasy. Getting into a strange car and going to a strange studio in downtown Los Angeles feels a bit intimidating. What if something goes wrong?

"Uh, I'm wondering if it's okay for me to bring my best friend, Michelle," I say suddenly. "You know, for moral support."

Now there's a dead silence and I'm worried that I've crossed some invisible line. Or maybe I've offended them.

"Well, some girls try that," Marcia says carefully, "but quite honestly, it never works out in their best interest. Having a friend with you on an interview and a photo shoot sends the wrong message to everyone. It gives us the impression that you're not confident and independent. It makes us question whether or not you're really cut out for modeling. It takes a strong person to become a model, Simi."

"That's right," Bryce says. "If you need a friend to come along and hold your hand, well, maybe you're not ready for this yet."

"No," I say quickly. "I'm ready. I just thought Michelle might enjoy it too."

"This isn't about entertaining our friends," Marcia says firmly. "It's about hard work and dedication. Perhaps you're not prepared for the demands of the modeling industry."

"No," I say again. "I am ready. I really am. I'll be ready when the car comes. And I'll put everything I have into this."

"Good girl," Marcia says warmly. "Because that is exactly what it takes."

Relieved that I didn't blow this amazing opportunity, we end the phone call and I feel even more excited about tomorrow's appointment. I can tell that these guys believe in me, and I understand their concern about me needing Michelle to hold my hand. And really, why would I want Michelle hanging around the agency? Knowing her, she'd be questioning everyone and everything and probably humiliating me. No, I do not want her to rain on my parade.

As I go through my closet, trying to decide what I'll wear to this life-changing photo shoot and interview tomorrow, I consider my mom. Naturally, I'll tell her about what I'm doing. But what if she plays the mom-card and starts questioning everything? Even worse, what if she insists on going there with me? Not that she can get off work. But what if she did get off work and marched in there with me? Would I be comfortable having my fashion-challenged mom sitting through all this with me? And what about what Marcia and Bryce said about independence? Besides that, Mom is always telling me how much she appreciates my independence. She encourages it.

No, this is something I need to do on my own. After all, I didn't drag Mom with me when I interviewed for a job at the yogurt shop a few weeks ago. I was bummed that I didn't get that job. But now I can see that it was probably just a blessing in disguise. Otherwise I wouldn't be about to interview for this opportunity with the modeling agency.

I know I need to do this myself, for myself. And I need to put my best foot forward and go into this interview with all the energy and enthusiasm I can muster. I will give this photo shoot my all, and I will succeed.

Mom is dirty and exhausted and almost two hours late when she comes home from work. She explains to me that she had to fix a flat tire on the side of the freeway. "No one even stopped to help," she says angrily as she plods down the hall to her room.

"That's terrible," I say.

"I'm beat." She pauses by her door. "I'm going to take a shower and just crash for a while. And don't worry about dinner. I'll just fix something later."

"I made spaghetti. There's leftovers in the fridge."

She gives me a weary nod. "Thanks, honey. You're a good girl."

I feel so sorry for her as she goes into her room. It's like nothing is going right for her these days. More than ever, I want to get this modeling job. I want to start bringing home money to help out with expenses. Somehow I must convince Marcia and Bryce that I am really the girl for the job. I've got to make them believe in me.

Once again, I'm checking my e-mail and Facebook, curious to see if any of the other agencies have responded to my portfolio. To my dismay, no one besides TMA has replied. But then

I remember what they said about how they like to jump in before others get the chance. And really, that seems smart. If I ran a modeling agency, I think I'd do the same thing.

I've been avoiding Michelle these past couple of days. Not that I've purposely ignored her calls, but when I noticed she'd called, I didn't call her back. And when she texted me, I texted her back but tried to sound busy and preoccupied. Finally, it's about nine and she calls and, feeling guilty, I answer.

"Hey, Michelle, what's up?"

"What's up is that you're already starting to act like a snobby supermodel. What's the deal anyway?"

"I'm sorry. I've just been busy."

"Busy doing what?"

So I explain that I have an appointment with TMA tomorrow. I tell her I have to be ready for it. I even throw in the bit about Mom and her flat tire. I'm not even sure why. Maybe I want her to feel sorry for me. After all, Michelle lives in a pretty nice house in a secure neighborhood. Shouldn't she have a little sympathy for someone like me?

"Even so, it feels like you're pushing me aside, Simi. Like you've already moved into your new life of being a model. Like you don't even need me anymore."

"I'm sorry, Michelle. You know that's not true. You're my best friend. I'll always need you. It's just that I really need to do this, too." Now I decide to get really honest with her. "Mom and I are barely making it on her salary, and now she's worried she'll get laid off. And you know my dad doesn't help out a bit. So if I can get modeling work, it might be our way out of this."

"Oh . . . yeah . . . I guess I never thought of it like that."

"That's because you have normal parents, Michelle. Sometimes I think you don't know how lucky you are."

"Yeah . . . maybe so."

"Anyway, if you think about it, why don't you pray for me tomorrow. Pray that the people at TMA really like me. Pray that I get this job." I tell her about how they have this campaign where they want "good" girls. "I mean, I got the impression they wanted to be sure I'd made a purity pledge or something."

"Seriously?"

"Maybe it's for a church or Christian organization."

"I suppose that's encouraging." She laughs. "Well, unless this organization is looking for virgins to sacrifice. You know, like they plan to throw you into a volcano to appease some pagan god or something."

I can't help but laugh. "Yeah, right. I'm sure that's what this is all about."

She asks me what I'm wearing and I tell her that I plan to wear my choir dress. "It's kind of like an LBD."

"A what?"

"A little black dress," I explain.

"Oh . . . I get it. Yeah, I guess that will look nice." And now she suggests some accessories that I might want to try with it, and I promise to text her from the agency to let her know how the interview's going. And before we finally hang up, she wishes me good luck and she sounds sincere. Michelle may be a skeptic, but she's still my best friend and I know she has my best interests at heart.

I'm so excited about tomorrow that it's impossible to get to sleep, so I do some Internet surfing, reading up about professional models and the industry in general, in the hopes that I'll learn how to speak their language before my big day. As I'm reading that the secret to one model's success is drinking lots of water, eating fresh fruit and veggies, and getting plenty of sleep,

I finally realize that it's after midnight. What if I show up looking tired and pasty with bags under my eyes tomorrow? So I force myself to go to bed, and counting backward from a thousand, I finally feel myself falling asleep.

When I wake up, it's almost nine thirty and Mom has already left for work. I feel a little guilty that I never got to tell her about today's appointment, but there's no time to worry about that now. I have only an hour to get myself completely ready for this important day. Feeling like I'm on fast speed, I hurry to get my hair and makeup right and then I put on the sleeveless black dress, and to my relief it looks rather sophisticated. Very Audrey Hepburn. And I'm sure Mrs. Norbert would approve.

Also, I've been practicing walking and sitting, and I really feel like I'm ready. I follow Michelle's advice and keep the accessories simple. Just my silver locket and my fake diamond-stud earrings. But to give this outfit a little zing, I put on the red high-heeled shoes, and the effect is just right. If this doesn't wow Marcia and Bryce, then maybe I'm just not cut out for this biz.

With my faux Kate Spade purse, which is the same shade of red as my shoes, I stand outside the apartment complex, feeling a bit conspicuous and overdressed. But thankfully, the black SUV, just like Marcia described yesterday, pulls up and a tall man wearing a dark jacket steps out. "You must be Miss Simi Fremont." He smiles at me, revealing a shiny gold tooth.

"Yes," I say nervously. "I am."

"And I'm Rod. Your driver today." He opens the back door, takes a little bow, then waves for me to go inside. Feeling very much like a princess, I climb into the vehicle. It's a late-model SUV with leather upholstery, tinted windows, and video players behind both front seats. An expensive ride, but nice.

Music plays quietly and Rod doesn't say anything as he

drives me through town and then onto the freeway, and although I consider making small talk with him, I'm not sure about the proper protocol with a driver. Instead I just lean back and enjoy the ride. I could so get used to this.

When he exits the freeway, I'm not exactly sure where we are and I didn't notice the signs, but it doesn't seem like we're in Los Angeles yet. And now I'm surprised to see that he's driving through what looks like a run-down industrial neighborhood. "Is the studio around here?"

"It's not too far."

As he continues down a street that doesn't look the least bit stylish, an uncomfortable rush of panic surges through me. Where am I? And who is this dude? Something feels wrong here. *What if I'm being kidnapped?*

Then I tell myself to stop being paranoid and ridiculous. Rod is just taking me to the agency. Maybe it's a shortcut. Michelle has probably had too much influence on me over the years. She always thinks the boogeyman is around the next corner. But as I survey the graffiti and trash Dumpster and some beat-up cars, I'm not the least bit reassured. What is going on?

"This seems an odd location for a modeling agency," I venture in a hesitant voice. "Or is this a shortcut?"

"Don't worry," he says lightly. "They use this big warehouse to do their photo shoots and screen tests and all that stuff that takes a lot of room. Kind of like a film lot, you know?"

"Oh . . ." I try to wrap my head around this. I suppose it makes sense. When Mom and I toured Universal Studios, some of the back lots didn't look that much different than this. I relax a little but still feel wary.

He turns into what seems to be an alley now. "The warehouse is cheaper, too. You know how downtown LA rent can be.

Anyway, their real offices are in this swanky high-rise down-town. They'll probably take you there after you finish your photo shoot. I heard they're having a special lunch catered for you girls."

"Oh, yeah . . . that sounds nice." I nod, feeling reassured at the mention of other girls. Except that now I feel nervous. What if the other girls have real experience? What if I blow the photo shoot?

He stops the SUV in front of a big, white cement-block building, and pushing the button on what looks like a garage-door opener on his visor, he waits for the big metal door to roll up and then drives the SUV into what looks like a dark hole compared to the bright sunlight out here.

"We have to do off-street parking," he says as the door goes down behind us. "To keep people from messing with our cars."

I'm not sure why, but as the garage door goes down, my heart starts to pound wildly. And now the feeling that some-thing is wrong grows even stronger. I don't know what or why or how, but all my instincts are telling me to run for my life. As I unbuckle the seat belt, I realize this might be an overreaction on my part, and yet somehow I know it's not. My instincts are yelling at me to get out of here.

I grab my purse, wishing I had my phone out and ready, and reach for the door handle. My plan is to casually step out of the car and look around and, if necessary, I'll bolt in whichever direction seems best. Except that it's so dark in here, I still can't see a thing. I give the door handle a tug and it's locked. I try and try, but I can't open it. I feel sick.

"Don't worry, Simi. I'll get the door for you."

"Oh . . . okay." I start to open my purse, but before my hand is inside, he reaches back and snatches it from me. "I'll take care of that for you."

"*What?*" My heart's pounding so hard, I can feel it in my ears. "What are you doing?"

"You need to understand the rules." He smiles, but it's a creepy smile, and his gold tooth gleams eerily in the green light coming from the dashboard.

"The rules?" My mouth is dry and my hands are starting to tremble.

"Yeah. When I let you out of the car, don't you even think about running." Now to my horror, he slips a shiny gunlike object out of his jacket and points it directly at me. "This might not look too intimidating, but trust me, a stun gun like this packs a big wallop. If you try to run or scream, it's gonna hurt. *A lot.* And you don't wanna get hurt, do you?" His grin is vile.

"What's going on?" I ask in a shaky voice. "Where are Marcia and Bryce? Why are you acting like this?"

He chuckles as he opens his door. "Don't you worry, pretty girl. You're about to meet the dynamic duo."

As he walks back to open my door, my mind is whirling. Fueled by fear and adrenaline, I must think of a way out. I've heard if you're abducted, your best hope of escape is to make a fast break before your captor gets you to an isolated place. But I'm already in an isolated place. All I can do is pray—*dear God, please, help me! Please, please, help me!*

The door jerks open and he reaches in to grab me by the arm, roughly pulling me from the car. "I know you wanna run or maybe scream for help." He shoves me in front of him, still holding tightly to my arm, twisting it behind my back so hard that I think my shoulder might dislocate. "They all think they can get away. But none of them make it." He twists my arm tighter. "Believe me, you won't be the first."

I stumble forward into the dark space with wobbly knees and teetering heels skidding on the cement. But he is holding on to my arm so firmly, it's like he's propelling me forward. It smells oily and dirty in here, like maybe this is an old garage. My head is spinning and I'm afraid I'm about to faint or throw up. Everything feels so unreal—like this is happening to someone else, or perhaps I'm starring in a horror movie.

Suddenly I wonder if all this might actually be a prank. Is this the agency's way of seeing what I'm really made of? As badly as I wish that were true, I know better.

This is for real.

My eyes have adjusted to the darkness, so I can see we're going toward a sliver of light that looks like the bottom of a door. When we reach the door, Rod stops and pulls something from his pocket, then grabbing my other arm, he binds my hands together behind my back. "Just to be safe," he tells me. And the next thing I know, he pulls a paper bag over my head.

"Are you going to kill me?" I ask desperately.

He chuckles evilly. "I hope it doesn't come to that."

This is only marginally reassuring. "What are—?"

"Shut up! If you want to survive this game, you better learn how to keep your mouth shut." And now I hear a door open and I'm shoved into another space. I can see light through the paper sack and I look down to see dirty yellow linoleum beneath my feet. It smells like old pizza and stale coffee in here.

"There you are," a woman says. "Right on time."

I can tell that it's Marcia, but it makes no sense.

"What are you doing to me?" I demand.

"*Shut up!*" Rod yells. "Didn't you hear what I said out there?"

"That's right." Marcia's voice remains smooth. "Children are meant to be seen and not heard."

"Well, this child is definitely worth seeing. Nice find, Marcia."

I recognize Bryce's voice, but I know better than to say anything now. Instead my mind is racing, trying to think of a way out of this hellish mess. Somehow I have to outsmart these creeps. But what are they doing? Why am I here? What is their game?

"Turn around," Marcia says.

I just stand there, not sure who she's talking to.

"I said *turn around*, you stupid girl," she snaps. *"Now!"*

Rod gives me a push and I slowly turn around, nearly stumbling over my own feet and wishing I hadn't worn high heels. I could so use some running shoes or steel-toed boots right now.

"She's got good legs," Marcia says.

"And a great bod," Bryce adds. "I like the little black dress, too. Nice and classy."

"Yeah. We could use some classy in this outfit." Marcia's laughter sounds vile.

"It's too bad," Bryce says. "She might've actually made a good model if she'd connected with a real agency."

"Bite your tongue," she tells him.

"Just saying."

"Don't even go there. As it is we should get top dollar for her. *Top dollar.*"

"Just make sure we keep her in good condition," Bryce says. "I mean you, Rod. Do not mess with her. No damage to her face. And no bruises, cuts, or scrapes. Do you understand?"

"Yeah, yeah, I got ya."

"At least until she meets Mr. T," Marcia injects. "We want to present the goods in tip-top shape."

"I think you should jack up the price," Bryce says. "Has Mr. T seen her photos yet?"

"He's seen them and approved. But I think you're right. A pretty little 'good girl' is a real rarity these days. I'll send him a message."

"Tell him we've got a bidding war going on."

"Yeah. Good idea."

"So you better keep her looking good until she's delivered," Marcia says. "If she's damaged in any way, not only will you not get paid, we will expect you to make it up to us. *Understand?*"

"I get it," Rod says. "I just don't get it now."

"After Mr. T, well, we'll just see how cooperative she wants to be," Marcia says this for my benefit I'm sure. "Even slightly used, she'll still be a valuable commodity."

"We have big plans for you, Simi," Bryce tells me. "However, you are no longer Simi Fremont."

"Give me her purse," Marcia says. I hear Rod walk across the room, and then I'm sure Marcia is going through my things. "Great. Here's her phone. We know about her mom and Trista and the twins. But we don't know Michelle's last name or where she lives yet. You get all that information."

"I'm already on it," Bryce says.

"Get rid of the ID. And dump the phone in the usual place."

"Yeah, yeah . . . hey, her girlfriend's last name is Diedericks. With an unusual name like that, it'll be a cinch to get her address."

"Why do you want *that?*" I demand.

"Who said you can talk?" Rod shoots back.

"Never mind," Marcia says. "And really, I don't care if she knows why we want this info. It's all a matter of security, Simi. We want to make sure you don't mess things up for us. Your mom and your friends are simply our insurance that you'll cooperate fully."

"If you care about their welfare, you'll do what you're told," Bryce adds.

"Are you threatening to — ?"

"It's all up to you," Marcia says in a calm but chilling tone. "Your mom and friends, even the dear little toddler twins — everyone will be just fine as long as you play along nicely. But trust me, doll face, the minute you break the rules, your mom and friends pay the price. *Do you get me?*"

I'm speechless. How can this be real? How can people be so evil?

"Do you get me?" she growls.

"Yes," I mutter. "I think so."

"Good. And don't think I'm not serious. Rod, maybe you can fill her in on how you're willing and able to carry out our orders."

"That's right. I got no problem going after your mom and your friends. Might even be fun. Especially if mom's a looker like you." He lets loose a wicked laugh that makes me feel like vomiting.

I can feel myself swaying now, getting dizzy. "I . . . need to sit — "

"Catch her!" Bryce yells.

I feel Rod grab me.

"Get her a chair," Marcia snaps.

I'm shoved down into a chair and I slump forward and the bag slips off my head. I remain down, pretending like I've fainted, but I'm peering through my hair that is over my face, seeing their feet as they hover around me.

Marcia has on ugly beige orthopedic-looking shoes and her ankles are swollen and pouring over the edges, which tells me she's older. And not exactly the fashion icon I'd imagined while talking on the phone yesterday. Bryce is wearing shiny black loafers and jeans, which leads me to believe he's somewhat more stylish and younger. They seem a strange pair.

They continue talking about how they plan to trick Mr. T with a bidding war as I sit slumped over. No one seems particularly concerned about me, but I can tell they just think I fainted. Finally I act as if I'm coming to, but before I can sit up, the paper bag is pushed onto my head again.

"Your new name is Serena Delray."

"What does that mean?"

"It means *from now on you will go by Serena*. How is that not clear?" Her voice drips in irritation. "Are you really that stupid?" She shoves my purse back into my lap. "Your new ID is in there. Not that you should need it. But just in case."

"We like to cover our bases," Bryce says.

"And now it's time for you to go," Marcia announces. "Rod? Please see Serena to her limo."

He chuckles. "You got it." Now he jerks me to my feet.

"Easy does it," Bryce says. "No bruises."

"Yeah, yeah." Rod is a little gentler as he pushes me to the door.

"Don't let us down, Serena," Marcia says. "Your dear mother and friends are counting on you."

"Bon voyage, Miss Delray," Bryce calls out cheerfully as Rod leads me out of the room and back into the dark garage. Bryce's farewell makes me wonder if I'm going on a boat. And if so, to where? Out of the country? As unbelievable as it is, I suspect I've fallen into some kind of human-trafficking scheme. I remember a woman who spoke at our school a couple of years ago. She talked about how human trafficking was on the rise and how it wasn't just foreigners and street kids anymore. But really, how can this be happening to me?

I hear what sounds like a metal door sliding open. "Step up," Rod tells me. "High."

I lift my foot but only hit my shin on hard metal. Rod cusses, then picks me up. I expect him to throw me into whatever this is, but instead he gently puts me down on what feels like a mattress and blankets. And then he slams the door shut.

The bag slips off my head, but it's even blacker in here than in the garage. I open and close my eyes, trying to adjust to the darkness, but it's useless. It's pitch black. And now I collapse on the musty-smelling blankets and just cry. I'm sure I'm in the back of a truck, and it's not long before I hear an engine start and eventually the truck is moving.

I try to gauge the time it takes to get out of the warehouse and how long it takes to get out of this sleazy neighborhood. And finally, when the truck stops at what I hope is a stoplight, maybe at an intersection where people could be outside and standing around, I get close enough to pound my feet on the door, and lying on my back, I kick it as loudly as I can and scream for help. Then the truck is moving again. Each time it comes to a stop I do this again. But eventually I can tell by the sound of the tires that we're on the freeway.

And now all I can do is pray. I pray and pray and pray. *God, please send the police to rescue me. And please make the truck break down or get a flat tire or run out of gas.* When that happens I will start banging on the metal door and screaming all over again. And hopefully someone will hear the noise and get curious.

What would I do if I heard sounds like that coming from a truck like this? Would I even notice? And if I did, would I do anything? I pray that whoever hears me will react and that they will call the police.

Praying is comforting, but eventually I tire of repeating the same words over and over again. So now I sing praise songs from our church. And then I repeat scriptures I memorized in youth group.

God is my lifeline and my anchor. God will get me out of this. I believe that he will rescue me. Hopefully before this day ends. Hopefully before I'm handed over to this nasty Mr. T person. I don't even want to imagine how horrible that would be. "God is my refuge and my strength," I say aloud, "my stronghold in a time of trouble."

Eventually my voice becomes hoarse from singing and praying and crying—and from thirst. It's hot in here . . . I'm guessing more than ninety degrees. And I'm so exhausted and thirsty that I feel myself drifting into sleep. But even as I'm slipping away, I'm holding on to God. He is my deliverer. I believe it.

I wake up to the sound of metal grinding, and it takes me a moment to figure out where I am and what happened. Then I blink into the bright sunlight, hoping to see policemen who will let me out of here and take me home. Instead, I see a wicked smile and a glistening gold tooth.

"Thought you might be thirsty," he tells me as he hands me a plastic cup.

I grab the cup and quickly drink the tepid water, and then he slams the door shut and it's not long until the truck is moving again. But it's not long before I feel like I'm getting dizzy, like everything is spinning, and I can tell something is wrong. Something was in that water I so eagerly gulped down.

I've been drugged. And now I feel myself slipping . . . tumbling . . . spiraling . . . down, down, down.

I wake up and, sitting up, I blink into the darkness, trying to remember where I am and how I got here. Oh yeah, the truck. And yet I don't feel any movement and it smells different. As my eyes adjust to the darkness, I glance around to see what looks like blinds over a window. I am in some sort of a room.

I stumble to my feet and fumble along the wall until I find a light switch by the door. I almost turn it on and then remember I am being held captive. I need to think carefully.

I quietly try the door and although the knob turns, the door does not budge. I feel above the doorknob to discover some kind of a lock. Probably a dead bolt, which I assume must only open from the outside.

I reach for the light switch again and then decide that, for now, I do not want to draw attention to myself. That means no lights. And no noise. I go over to the window and quietly peek through the plastic blinds. There are bars outside of the window. That's nothing unusual in the Los Angeles area. Most of the ground-level apartments in our complex have security bars.

I always assumed that bars were meant to keep criminals out of your house. Now I realize they can also be used to keep people in. There are spotlights outside, pointing away from the house and fully illuminating a fairly big backyard surrounded by shrubbery. And behind the bushes and trees I can spot parts of what looks like a tall metal security fence. It feels like I'm in some sort of a prison. As my eyes adjust to the darkness, I can see that this looks like a fairly typical bedroom. Not so different from mine at home.

Except I cannot get out.

Thinking of home fills me with both longing and anxiety. As much as I've complained about our cramped apartment, I would give anything to be there right now. Missing home makes me think of Mom. I hate to imagine how freaked she must be for me to disappear like this. How long have I been missing? Just overnight? Or was I drugged for longer than that? Does she have any way to know where I'm at or that I've been kidnapped by thugs claiming to be with Top Models and Actors Inc.? Are the police looking for me yet? Or will they treat me like a runaway and wait a few days before they respond? Oh, why didn't I tell her where I was going?

I inch my way across what feels like dirty carpeting until I reach the door again. I consider pounding on it just in case there's someone out there who might let me out. But I suspect the only ones out there are my captors. Or maybe it's Rod with the golden tooth and stun gun. Whoever is out there, I'm pretty sure I don't want to aggravate them in the middle of the night. Who knows what they might do to me? And what about Mr. T? What if this is his house? I really, really don't want to meet him. Just thinking of this monster fills me with terror.

My head is throbbing, probably from the drugs Rod slipped me, and my mouth feels as dry and gritty as sand. But the light coming in from the window gleams upon what appears to be a water bottle on the floor by the bed. I rush to get it, hoping it's not empty. To my relief it's full—but now I stop myself. What if it's drugged too?

I try the lid and the seal seems to be unbroken. But I'm so thirsty I'm not sure I care. I open the bottle and sample what tastes like ordinary water. Unable to control myself, I gulp it down. If it turns out to be drugged, I will simply escape into another long lapse of sleep, which could be a blessing. And maybe I'll wake up to find this has all just been the worst imaginable nightmare ever.

· · · · · · · · · ·

The next time I wake up, it's daylight outside. I have no idea what time it is, but it feels like early morning. I look around the drab room. The walls and carpet are dirty beige, the color of dust. The bed consists of a bare mattress on the floor with a cheap blanket and a stained pillow that is so gross looking, I cannot believe I slept on it. Around the mattress, on the carpet and the walls, are nasty-looking stains. I don't even want to think about what might've caused them.

There are no other furnishings in the room and, besides the closet, which other than a couple of plastic hangers is empty, there is only the door and the window to break the monotony of the bare, scarred walls. I go to look more closely at the window now, thinking perhaps I can open it and at least yell loud enough to get the attention of neighbors. That is, if there are any neighbors.

I can't see any other houses from my vantage point. But I quickly discover that the window's bolted tightly shut. From the outside. There's no way to open it. How difficult would it be to break this window? If I could get a hole in it somehow, I might be able to scream loud enough to draw some attention. Unless I just draw the wrong kind of attention.

I begin frantically pacing, trying to decide what to do, but the harder I think, the more confused I feel. Suddenly, I remember the first-aid class I took last year. One of the first things our instructor taught us was "don't panic." Of course, I'm not sure how this applies to my situation. *How can I not panic?*

Still, I remember how he explained that if your brain surrenders to terror, it impedes blood flow and you stop thinking clearly. For that reason I take several deep breaths and attempt to calm myself. Now I try to remember more tips from that class. We were told to assess the situation and prioritize needs. We were also taught not to do anything to make matters worse. Perhaps like breaking the window.

Suddenly, breaking the window seems like my best hope. It's possible that this house is located near others. If I can make enough noise to get someone's attention, I might have a chance. I go back to the window, staring out onto what seems a surprisingly well-maintained yard. Other than being a little overgrown with trees and bushes along the perimeter, it seems fairly green and the lawn looks healthy. This isn't the norm for Los Angeles area backyards. Of course, I'm probably not anywhere near LA now.

I stand on tiptoe, trying to peer out beyond the vegetation, but it's impossible to see if neighbors are nearby. Still, I wonder if it might be worth a try to break the window and cry for help. I'm looking around the room for something solid enough to break glass. I consider my high-heeled shoes or even better, the heavy metal latch on my purse. I pick it up and practice giving it a nice, hard whirl around and around. If I can just swing it hard enough, I might succeed. Just then the door opens and

I stop my purse in midswing and pretend to be looking inside it, although the only thing there is my empty wallet with the stupid fake ID.

"Oh . . . you're already up," the girl says without much interest as she looks around my room with curiosity.

I stare at her. Who is she and why is she here? I'm guessing she's about my age, but there's a definite hardness about her. And it's not just that her short-cropped hair has been dyed jet black, or that she has a pierced lip, or even the creepy tattoo of a large black snake slithering up her right arm.

"Who are you?" I ask with a timid smile. I'm hoping against hope that she's come to set me free.

"Tatiana." She comes closer to me now, peering curiously at me as if I'm the specimen in the bottom of a petri dish. Suddenly I'm aware that I'm still wearing my black choir dress, which is wrinkled and dirty. It hurts to remember how I convinced myself I looked so sophisticated in my LBD. So certain that I was going to make a great impression on Marcia and Bryce as I launched my new modeling career. How could I have been so stupid and naive?

"And you're Serena, right?"

Reminded of my new identity, I simply nod. She's so close I can smell her breath and it's rancid like rotten meat, but I try not to react. "So, Tatiana, do you think you can get me out of here?" I quietly ask. And I'm about to offer her money, although I have no idea where I'll get it, but it seems worth a shot. "If you do I can—"

"*No way*," she cuts me off, scowling darkly. "Don't even go there."

"Oh . . . okay . . ." A discouraged sigh slips out.

"But I can get you some breakfast." She's staring at my red

high heels over by the bed, gazing longingly at them as if she'd like to try them on. Perhaps they can be a useful bargaining tool . . . in time.

While she's checking out my shoes, I cautiously move toward the door, which I assume isn't locked. "Can I go out and—?"

"Back off!" In one quick move, she snatches my purse from me and leaps between me and the door. "I'll take *that*." She's already got the red bag open and is pawing through it like she thinks she'll find something valuable.

"But it's mine."

"Not anymore." Standing like a barricade in front of the door, she glares at me with a doubled fist just inches from my face. "Watch your step, girlfriend."

"Marcia and Bryce said I'm not supposed to get any bruises." I try to keep my voice calm, hoping to reason with her.

"Yeah well, I take my orders from Jimmy." She opens the door. "Stay put and you won't get hurt."

"Please, wait, Tatiana." I stay frozen in place, trying to think of a way out. "I, uh, I need to use the bathroom."

"Oh, why didn't you say so?" She narrows her eyes. "But I'm warning you, Serena, don't try anything stupid. Jimmy's out there and all I have to do is holler and he'll back me up. And hey, if we have to give you some bruises, we'll make sure to put them where they won't show."

"I just want to use the bathroom. I won't give you any trouble. I promise."

She tips her head toward the hallway. "Come on then."

Now she leads me two doors down, opens another door, and nods into what appears to be a fairly normal, albeit filthy, bathroom. "There you go. Knock yourself out."

As soon as I'm in the bathroom, she firmly closes the door and the lock clicks. There must be another dead bolt — on the outside of the door. And just like the bedroom, I can see the outline of bars on the frosted window. When I try to open it, I find that it's bolted closed.

Although I'm too dehydrated to really need to use the toilet, I stay in here awhile, studying the room in case there's something I'm missing, like an attic opening or loose floorboards or something. But since it all seems fairly tight, I simply flush the toilet for effect and then take my time to wash my hands and my face and drink from the faucet. However I do not use the disgusting excuse for a towel. I hope to never be that desperate.

I knock on the door and after a few minutes, Tatiana returns. "So, do you want some breakfast or not?"

"Yeah. Mostly I'm just really thirsty." I try to peer down the hallway to see who or what is in the rest of the house, but Tatiana pushes me back toward the room I slept in.

"You're supposed to stay in your room until Jimmy says you can come out."

"Who's Jimmy?" I ask as she escorts me back.

"He takes care of us." Her unexpected smile makes her seem slightly more human. "He's a good guy."

I want to ask her if she's crazy but figure that won't endear me to her, and somehow I've got to make this girl like me. "Are you here because you *want* to be here?" I ask before she closes my door.

She shrugs. "There are worse places."

"Yeah, but — "

The door slams in my face and the dead bolt clanks loudly. End of conversation. I look around the sparse room and wish I'd thought to take my empty water bottle to the bathroom to refill. Who knows when I'll get another drink? Although Tatiana did say she'd bring me breakfast, didn't she? I look around my room to see that not only is my purse gone but my shoes are missing too. So much for using them to barter with later. I obviously have no rights whatsoever in this place.

I wait for what feels like hours for Tatiana to return. Did I only imagine she said she was bringing me breakfast? Today? I look out the window and, judging by the short shadows, I figure it must be past noon by now. This room is stuffy and stale and I grow thirstier and hungrier as the day wears on. What if Tatiana forgot about me? What if I'm left here forever?

I return to the window, peering out and wishing I could see a house or even someone passing by. But the only signs of life are birds that are busily plucking at the tiny red berries on an overgrown bush. This simply reminds me that I haven't eaten since yesterday morning. Was it only yesterday? Or did I lose more time than that while under the influence of whatever was slipped to me in the truck?

I bang my fist against the window, wondering how hard I must pound to break the glass or if that's even possible. Then I imagine my fist going right through and severing a main artery. Would anyone come to my aid? Probably not. Besides, even if I could break the glass, what good is it if no one is outside to hear me? Plus I remember Tatiana's warning that she and Jimmy will hurt me in places where bruises won't show. Apparently Marcia's concerns about "not damaging the goods" mean nothing to these brutes. But maybe they need a reminder. If there's a real cash value attached to me, perhaps I can get more respect. Do I have the nerve to mention this . . . or would it only make my situation worse?

I start pounding on the door now, yelling that I need to use the bathroom and that I'm dying of thirst. I wait a few minutes, hoping someone will take pity on me. But no one comes. I try again and this time I press my ear to the door and listen, but I don't hear a thing. Finally, I can't contain my emotions anymore, and I burst into tears and fall onto the nasty mattress and just cry myself to sleep.

I wake to the sound of someone entering the room. It's Tatiana again and she's got a bag from McDonald's. "Still hungry?" she asks as if she doesn't care.

"Yes," I mutter as I stumble to my feet. "And thirsty."

She looks unconcerned. "Sorry, I forgot to get you a drink. Oops."

I hold up my water bottle. "Please, can I fill this?"

She shrugs and holds out her hand.

Suspecting she'll disappear with it and never return, I tell her I need to use the bathroom. She looks doubtful but finally agrees to escort me down the hall where I attempt to use the toilet, but I am so dehydrated it's almost pointless. Once again I drink water from the tap, gulping as much as I can take in without making myself sick. And then I fill my water bottle. Satisfied that I might be able to make it through the night if I have to, I knock on the door, waiting for Tatiana to let me out. But not surprisingly, she doesn't come.

I sit on the edge of the tub, waiting for what feels like half an hour. And then I decide to use this opportunity to slug down more water, even though I don't really feel thirsty. But who knows when I'll get another chance? And right now my only focus is on survival. I'm just refilling my bottle when I hear the dead bolt snap open.

"Aren't you done yet?" she demands impatiently.

"Yeah. Sorry." I calmly put the lid back on the water bottle, controlling myself from pointing out that I banged on the door and waited for her. I need to be careful with this girl if I'm going to win her sympathy. And that's my goal. "Thanks for being patient."

She looks surprised. "Well, come on then."

"So, do you know how long I'll be locked in that room?" I ask in what I hope is a nonchalant tone. "I mean, it's kinda boring and it's not like I'm going to run away or anything."

"Right . . ." She looks skeptical as she holds the door to my jail cell open. "You expect me to fall for that one?"

I shrug. "Well, I'm guessing this place is locked up pretty tight."

With her hand on the knob, she studies me, then nods. "You got that right."

"But you're allowed to come and go?"

Now she glares at me. "Aren't you just full of questions."

"I'm just curious. Wouldn't you be too? I mean, if you'd just arrived and didn't know what to—"

"Shut up!" She swears at me as she shoves me back into the room and slams the door, snapping the dead bolt tight.

To my relief the McDonald's bag is still sitting on the floor by my bed, and even though the Egg McMuffin is cold and probably hours old, I'm grateful. And although I'm tempted to gobble it down, I remember to thank God and I even ask him to bless it, hoping that maybe he will multiply it, like Jesus with the loaves and fishes.

But when I open my eyes, it's still just one McMuffin. So I pace myself and eat slowly. Who knows when I'll see food again?

···[CHAPTER 8]················

I 've heard that solitary confinement messes with your mind, and I'm beginning to understand this. God made people to need people. My only human contact on my second day is when Tatiana, who doesn't even speak to me, drops off a box of dry cereal, a gallon of water, and a bucket. I try to engage her by asking what the bucket is for, but she silently slams the door in my face. And as the day wears on, with no bathroom breaks, I figure it out.

I press my ear against the door off and on during the day, but it's silent as a tomb out there. It sounds as if no one is here, and I begin to wonder if they've abandoned me completely. But I keep reminding myself that I'm not really alone. God is with me. I know it. I believe it. But all this solitude is taking its toll. My nerves are wearing thin, and I suppose my faith is wavering slightly as well.

As I'm crying out to God to rescue me, it occurs to me that I need to confess my own responsibility for my dire circumstances. So I get down on the grubby carpet, kneeling with hands lifted up, and attempt to confess my foolishness to God. As hard as it is to admit all my failings — and they are many — I know this is exactly what I need to do.

As I confess my stupid shallowness, I remember Mrs. Norbert's advice. She told me I wasn't ready. She cautioned me to wait for her to help me . . . and yet I ran ahead. I also remember how Michelle warned me to be careful. She told me about how people lie on the Internet. How did I respond to my best friend? I just laughed.

Even worse, I remember how I conveniently managed to keep the news about my agency interview from Mom. Although I didn't actually lie, I was deceptive by omission. I rationalized that it was only because I didn't want to worry her. But the truth was, I didn't *want* her to know. I was afraid she would insist on going to the appointment with me. I was worried that her presence there would humiliate me.

It sickens me to think of this now. How could I have been so stupid and so shallow and so deceptive? To think that my mother, who loves me and would do anything for me, would have embarrassed me in front of the likes of Marcia and Bryce isn't just absurd, it is insane. How I wish I could turn back the clock. How I wish I'd told her. Keeping my whereabouts a secret may well be the end of me. How could I have been so completely stupid?

"I'm sorry," I tell God. "I did it all wrong. Please forgive me. And if I ever get the chance to see Mom and Michelle and even Mrs. Norbert, I will confess this all to them, too. I will ask everyone to forgive me."

I continue to pour out my heart until I don't feel there's anything left to confess. And when I'm done, I know that God has forgiven me. But I still have no idea how he is going to get me out of this. The truth is, I know now that I don't deserve to be rescued. I am here because of my own foolishness. My personal vanity has allowed me to be lured into a trap.

When morning comes, I hear some noises in the house, but no one comes to my door. Although I continue to pray and believe God is with me, my loneliness is overwhelming. However, this time of isolation gives me time to think. If I'm going to get out of here, I will need a plan.

The first part of my plan is to somehow get Tatiana—or anyone else who lives in this house—to trust me. Somehow I've got to make them believe that I'm not going to run. If I can convince them that I'm trustworthy, it's possible I will get a little freedom. And if I can get a little freedom, it's possible that, with God's help, I will discover a way to escape.

However, to get people here to trust me, I will have to pretend to be like them. Which means I will have to be dishonest. I will have to hide my real feelings, my real reactions. Is keeping a secret like this deceitful? Or is it simply a clever means to escape from corrupt people?

Once again, I ask God to help me with this, and suddenly I feel compelled to pray for the others in this house. I start with Tatiana and then I pray for Jimmy, someone I've never met. And as I'm praying for them, my attitude starts to change. Yes, I may have to pretend I'm something I'm not, but now I care about the others. I'm curious as to how they came to be here. And I'm hoping and praying that as much as I help myself, I might be able to help them, too.

It's late afternoon when Tatiana comes into my room. She's holding out a paper plate with a couple pieces of pepperoni pizza on it, and grateful tears fill my eyes as I stand to greet her.

"I'm so glad to see you," I say as she hands me the grease-soaked paper plate.

"Yeah, yeah." She runs her fingers through her hair, making it look even spikier than usual.

"Thank you so much for this," I gush at her. "And please, don't go. I'm so lonely. Can't you stay and talk awhile?"

"Yeah, right. We have so much to talk about." She rolls her eyes and I notice she's changed her clothes and is wearing makeup. Instead of her gray tank top and cutoffs, she has on a short, strapless red-and-black striped dress—and my red heels.

"You look really nice," I tell her, containing my irritation that she's wearing the only shoes I have. "Big date tonight?"

She laughs with cynicism. "Yeah . . . several."

"What day is it?" I try to prolong this encounter.

"Last I heard it was Saturday." Without turning her back on me, she reaches for the doorknob. "Later." And then she's gone.

I try to process how long I've been gone now. I went to the appointment with Marcia and Bryce on Tuesday. I was drugged that night in the truck . . . and several days here . . . I count the days on my fingers: five days. But it feels more like five years. The only encouraging thing is that the police must be looking for me by now. But would they have any idea where I am? Do I? Based on the greenness of the backyard and trees, I suspect I've been taken up north. But I have no idea where. Oregon, Washington, Canada, Alaska?

I look down at the pizza and, once again, I thank God for this meal and I ask him to bless it and keep me from food poisoning, since, like the McMuffin, it's just room temperature and for all I know it could've been sitting out for days. I sniff it and my stomach rumbles so I go ahead and take a bite.

As I slowly eat, I must admit my faith is wavering a little. It's hard to believe it's been five days. I truly expected to be out of this mess by now. But at the same time I am extremely thankful that nothing worse than solitary confinement has happened to me. And I'm thankful that I can keep crying out to God, and I'm still trying to trust that he's going to rescue me.

Throughout the day, I have heard the sounds of what I first thought were guns and then later realized were actually fireworks. The frequency of the noises seems to increase into the night. And then it hits me: Today's the Fourth of July. Of course, the irony of this does not escape me. I am celebrating Independence Day by being locked up and held prisoner. Surely this is a Fourth of July I will never forget.

. . . .

Late in the night I'm awakened by a lot of door slamming and bashing going on somewhere in the house. I try to block out the noise by singing to myself, but eventually I hear someone screaming in pain and it's impossible to ignore. It sounds like one of the girls is being beaten. I pray for her until the screaming stops and the house grows quiet again — deathly quiet.

Somehow I manage to fall back to sleep. But when morning comes, I feel like I am climbing the walls. Literally. It's like I need to do something to purge the sounds from last night from my head. So I start doing handstands. I used to be in gymnastics, back in middle school before I got too tall.

To distract myself from the madhouse I'm imprisoned in, I try all sorts of old tricks, sometimes crashing and bashing around so loudly I'm surprised Tatiana doesn't come in and tell me to shut up. I think I understand why these walls are so scratched and scuffed and banged now. Trapped animals tend to claw at their cages.

I can't believe that just one week ago I went to early church with Mom. Or how we stopped by Rosie's Deli to get a quick breakfast afterward. What would I give for a meal like that now? I'm also ashamed to think of how I griped and groaned about having to babysit that day. What wouldn't I do to be babysitting Leo and Lacy instead of being here? Maybe we really don't know what we have until it's gone.

But to distract myself I continue with my old gymnastic moves and am in the middle of a back bend when the door opens. Pulling myself up into a standing position, I'm surprised to see a blond guy gaping at me like he's seeing an apparition. I make a dramatic bow and then smile broadly.

"Not bad," he tells me.

"Well, now thank you, thank you very much," I say in a corny Elvis imitation.

"I just wanted to make sure you were okay. I heard the noise."

"Sorry about that. I was just really, really restless." I continue babbling away about nothing, willing to do anything, including acting like the village idiot, to delay his exit for as long as possible. That's how hungry I am for human companionship — as well as food. "So what happened to Tatiana? I haven't seen her lately."

"She's, uh, sleeping it off."

"Oh." I nod like this is no surprise. "So, are you going to let me out of my cage now?" I smile hopefully, remembering my plan to win his trust.

He presses his lips together, rubbing his chin, as if he's actually considering my request.

"I promise to be on my best behavior." I smooth out my permanently wrinkled and probably ruined black dress.

"I almost believe you."

"So, are you Jimmy? The one Tatiana says takes such good care of us?"

He nods. "That's me."

I stick out my hand and he shakes it. "Nice to finally meet you. Are you friends with Marcia and Bryce too?"

"Yeah . . . you could say that. Business associates at least."

I study him closely. Dressed in a plaid western shirt and holey blue jeans, he's about my height or maybe even shorter and somewhat slight in build. My best guess is that he's late teens to early twenties. His hair appears to be naturally brown but has been highlighted to look blondish. He's actually pretty good looking. But like Tatiana, there's a toughness in his steely blue eyes. Or maybe it's just sadness. I silently send up a prayer for him.

"Well, I'm willing to let you out, Serena. But I'm warning you, if you try to pull anything, I guarantee you, you'll be sorry."

I force another smile. "I give you my word. You can trust me."

He shrugs. "Yeah, well, I've been around long enough to know that people sometimes say things they don't mean."

"I just want to be with people." At least that's not a lie.

"Okay. But you mess with me and you'll be sorry." He gives me a hardened look. "Marcia and Bryce might want you to look good for Mr. T, but I can make your life miserable until then — without leaving any marks."

"Yeah, I'm sure you can." I let out a weary sigh. "But honestly, I'm just lonely and I'm going stir crazy. I promise to be good if you let me out."

"All right." He steps aside now and waves to the open door. "Just so you know, all the windows are locked and barred. We have dead bolt locks on all the doors. And I control the keys."

He pulls out what looks like a bulky iPhone from his pocket. "You know what this is?"

"A phone?"

He chuckles as he points it at me. "It does send a powerful message."

"Huh?"

"It's a Taser."

"What?"

"A stun gun."

"Oh." I nod like this is no big deal. "It doesn't look like the one Rod had. His looked more like a gun. Kind of a sci-fi gun."

Jimmy's brows lift slightly. "Did Rod have to use it on you?"

I shake my head. "No way. I was a perfect little lady for him."

"Okay." He slips it back into his shirt pocket and snaps the pocket closed. "You just keep that up and we won't have any problems then."

It feels strange to follow him out of the room. As we pass the bathroom, I ask him if I can use it and he just shrugs. "Sure, whatever."

"And would it be okay if I took a shower too? It's been almost a week and—"

"Yeah, no problem. We don't expect you to be all stinky and gross."

"Thanks." Now I look at my sad little black dress and frown. "I don't suppose there's any chance I could get a fresh change of clothes?" I ask hopefully. "I mean, I don't want to sound whiny, but—"

"I'll ask one of the girls to find you something."

I thank him, curious as to the other girls. I go into the bathroom where, to my surprise, he doesn't even lock the door once

I'm inside. I consider locking it from my side, but why bother since I'm sure he can get in if he wants to? Besides, it would probably only make him suspicious. Why rock this boat?

It feels like such a luxury to take a shower and wash my hair. I help myself to the bath products and take my time to scrub off what feels like layers of filth and grime. Then I dig around in a messy linen cabinet until I find a clean towel. I'm just drying myself off when I notice the small pile of clothes next to the sink. It's not much. Just athletic shorts and a baggy T-shirt and a pathetic pair of underwear and a bra, but at least they look and smell clean. Or cleaner than my sad little dress.

After I'm dressed, and since no one is knocking on the door yet, I take a few minutes to wash out my dress and my under-wear. I'm hoping I can dry them in front of the window in my room, and I'm just rinsing the soap out when a petite girl walks in. She has shoulder-length hair that has been dyed magenta and is in need of a good conditioning treatment. As she gets closer to me, I can see that the roots are brown, just like her eyes.

"What're you doing?" She frowns curiously at my hands in the sink of murky-looking water.

I give her a smile as I lift the dripping black dress. "I'm just washing my clothes."

"You know, we do have a laundry room for that."

"Oh?" I nod. "Good to know." I'm being extra friendly, hoping to win this girl's trust. She's very petite and seems a little younger than me. "But this dress is supposed to be hand washed anyway." I study the poor misshapen garment, wondering if it will ever be useable again. "This was my choir dress in high school."

"You were in choir?" Her big eyes brighten with interest. "Are you a good singer?"

I shrug as I squeeze water out. "I'm okay."

She's sitting on the counter now, kicking her heels as she watches me finishing up my washing. "I was never in choir or anything like that," she says wistfully, "but I do love to sing."

"Are you any good?"

Just like that, she breaks into a Katy Perry song, and although she's a little off-key, her enthusiasm is genuine. So I smile and tell her that she sings beautifully. Really, what can it hurt?

"Thanks." She grins. "You're Serena, right?"

I nod. "What's your name?" I grab another towel to wrap my dress and underthings in so they won't drip all over the floor.

"Ruby." She hops down from the counter. "Ruby Red."

I blink. "Really? *Ruby Red?*"

She laughs. "Well, you know."

And then I realize that, like me, she's been assigned a fake name. "Yeah . . . I know." I hold up my wet laundry. "I'm going to put these in my room to dry." But now I'm worried I might get locked up again, so as I go down the hallway, I continue talking to her about music and singing. I'm hoping I can entice her to follow me. At least if I go into lockdown, I'll have company. "*American Idol* is one of my favorite shows," I say as I go into my room.

"Yeah, me too. And I used to dream about being on it someday," she admits as I'm putting my soggy dress on one of the hangers.

"That's cool," I say as I hook the hanger over the top of the blinds, hoping the sun from the window will dry it.

"I guess that won't be happening though."

"Why not?" I arrange my underwear on the other hanger, hooking it on the blinds too. "You can keep auditioning until you're twenty-eight. And I'll bet you're not even old enough to try out yet."

"Yeah. I'm just fourteen." She stops herself like she's given out too much information.

"It's okay. It's not like I'll tell anyone."

She looks relieved.

"You shouldn't give up your dreams," I say. "And you should keep on singing, too."

"Really? You think I have talent?"

"I think you have a sweet voice and you should keep working on it." At least that was honest. "Maybe we can sing together sometime."

"Yeah, that'd be cool."

"So, how long have you been here?" I use my fingers to comb my damp hair.

Her brow creases. "You mean here in this house?"

I shrug, trying to figure this out as I go. "Yeah, whatever."

"We all came to this house in May, I think it was."

"Oh . . ." I try not to act too interested since I know everyone here is pretty tight-lipped. I just act like I'm making conversation.

"We were all in different places before coming here."

"All? You mean besides Jimmy and Tatiana?"

"Yeah, the other girls."

"Oh, yeah. So you've only been together a couple months . . ."

"Well, I've known Jimmy longer than that. About a year I guess. Maybe a little more."

"Uh-huh." I try not to look shocked, but I assume she was only thirteen when she got stuck in this lifestyle. "How did you, uh, come to be here?"

"It was pretty messed up at home. At least my mom's

boyfriend was messed up, you know what I mean?" She peers curiously at me.

"Yeah." I nod like I get this—and I think I do. "That sucks."

"Tell me about it. He's a total loser who thinks he can use me the same way he's using my mom. So one day I was fed up with the jerk. And I confronted my mom and I was like, 'It's him or me, Mom. You gotta choose.'"

I shake my head sadly. "And . . . ?"

She looks down at her feet. "She chose him. Duh."

"I'm sorry." I place a hand on her shoulder. "That's so wrong."

"Yeah. So then it was like, what do I do? I stayed with a friend for a while. But then her mom was going to report everything to CPS. So I was like see ya later. And then I was on the streets and it wasn't so bad since it was summer. And a lot of kids were homeless."

"So you kinda banded together?" I'm trying to wrap my head around this.

"Yeah. But the weather started getting cold. So some of us came out here and that was better for a while. But then it started getting pretty rough. And I didn't really know anyone and I was ready to just give up."

"Did you ever think about going home?"

"I called my mom's phone and the jerk answered and I just hung up."

"Oh."

"That's when Jimmy found me."

"Oh . . . yeah." I nod like this makes sense, like I can totally relate.

"Jimmy was the first one to really help me. He had money and he gave me clothes and food and stuff." She shrugs. "He gave me a place to stay. Sure, it wasn't much, but it was better than being on the streets. Especially in the winter."

"So winter is pretty cold up here?" I'm hoping she'll divulge where we are. "I mean, colder than LA. That's where I'm from."

"Yeah, I'm pretty sure Portland is a lot colder than LA." She smiles. "That's cool you're from LA. I've always wanted to go there. That's where I thought I was headed, but then I stayed here instead."

So I tell her a little about LA and then ask about where she came from. She lets it slip out that she's from Idaho, but that's all. I can tell she's worried about giving too much information.

"Well, I've never been in Portland before," I say before she can get too concerned. "But I've heard it's really pretty up here."

"Oh, yeah, for sure. There's lots of trees and some pretty gardens Jimmy took us to once. Portland's pretty cool."

"You don't miss Idaho then?"

She shakes her head. "Sometimes . . . I guess . . . I mean, if things were different."

"So, it's your choice to be here?" I ask tentatively. "And if you wanted to leave, you could?"

She frowns. "Well, I owe Jimmy a lot, you know." She waves her hand around this dismal room. "I mean, this house is a lot better than where I was living. I know it's not cheap. And he's put out a lot of money for me. So I have to earn my keep, you know?"

"Yeah, I know." Does she honestly believe she owes anyone anything? Doesn't she get that she's still a juvenile and that no kid should be forced to live like this? Like she's owned by Jimmy or something?

"Anyway, Jimmy keeps telling me things will get better here. If we just give it time."

"Yeah . . ." Again I pretend to understand although I feel like screaming. If I'm going to get anywhere with these people,

I'll have to practice patience. "Sometimes we just need to wait, huh? For life to improve."

She bravely tells me that we should never give up hope. But I wonder how long she will have to wait for her life to get better. And what if her hope gets extinguished before then? Or what if she doesn't survive? What if I don't? And how can I keep up this pretense, faking it by acting like this bizarre lifestyle is acceptable and like I am here by choice?

CHAPTER 9

"What are you doing in here, Ruby?" Tatiana pushes the door fully open and steps into my room.

"Just talking to Serena."

Tatiana frowns at me now. "Who unlocked this door?"

"Jimmy," I tell her.

"Really?" Her eyes narrow as if she doubts this.

"Yeah. He let me out and I took a shower and then someone brought me these clothes." I wave my hand down at my outfit, acting like it's something much nicer than ugly castoffs I would normally not want to be caught dead in.

"That was me," Ruby says proudly. "I got them from Kandy since Jimmy said you were bigger than me. Or else I would've loaned you some of my clothes. And something cuter than those." She wrinkles her nose at my outfit.

"Well, at least they're clean," I tell her. "I didn't get a chance to pack anything before I came." What an understatement.

"I'm going to ask Jimmy," Tatiana tells me, "to make sure you're really supposed to be out roaming around the house. I thought we were keeping you locked up until your hot date with Mr. T." She laughs like this is really humorous and not totally disgusting.

As Tatiana leaves, Ruby tosses me a look that's a mixture of curiosity and concern. "Is that true? You're the one they brought here for Mr. T?"

I just nod.

"And now they're waiting to find out how much he's going to pay for you?"

I take in a breath. "Yeah, I guess so."

"I heard it's going to be a lot of money. It sounds like the price keeps going up."

"Well, that should make everyone happy." I say this in my most nonchalant tone. "So, everyone here knows all about Mr. T then?"

Ruby nods, but her expression is slightly suspicious now.

"Have you met him too?"

She shakes her head. "No way. He only goes for a *certain* kind of girl."

"Yeah." I conceal my disgust. "I know all about that."

"And you're okay with it?"

"Sure," I lie. "Marcia said it's like paying my dues."

Ruby looks surprised. "He does pay a lot of money for, uh, for girls like you. But usually they're not real pleased about meeting Mr. T."

I hold up my hands. "Hey, don't get me wrong. I'm not particularly pleased about it either. The truth is, I'm pretty scared. But it's not like I have a choice."

"Yeah, well, who does?" I can tell by her expression that she's unsure about me now. Somehow I've got to win this girl over. For both our sakes.

So I tell her that my mom was about to get laid off and that she couldn't afford to take care of both of us. And I can tell it's working because Ruby seems like she's trusting me again. I do feel guilty for keeping my true feelings and motives a secret from this girl, but at the same time, it's the only way I can help her and myself. And based on what little I know of her, I become even more determined to do this. Maybe that's part of the reason I'm here.

"Most of Mr. T's girls never come back to stay with us," she informs me with a somber expression.

"Why is that?"

She shrugs. "Don't know."

"Do you know where they go to?"

She looks away, and I can tell she doesn't want to tell me.

"What if I *want* to come back here?"

She turns back to me. "Would you?"

"Why not?"

Just then Tatiana returns. "Jimmy wants to see you now." Then she waits, watching as I head out of the room.

"Where is he?" I pause in the hallway.

"The basement." Tatiana says this like I should know.

"Where's that?"

"I'll show you," Ruby offers.

"No," Tatiana snaps at her. "You're not needed down there. Go to your room, little girl."

Ruby looks hurt but doesn't say anything. Instead she continues walking, leading the way to a great room with several mismatched couches and a big-screen TV. Off to one side is a large but messy kitchen, and numerous bottles of liquor line the counters. Ruby turns toward a stairway and quietly goes up. I assume her room is up there. But my eyes are searching around this space, taking inventory of the windows and doors. All appear to be barred or else protected by metal exterior doors that look very secure.

"This way." Tatiana shoves me past the kitchen and into an alcove where she opens a door. "Down there."

I go down the dimly lit stairs and enter into a space carpeted in brown, giving this room an even gloomier appearance. It smells slightly damp down here, like mold and mildew and something else I don't want to think about. There are no windows down here. But like upstairs, there is a big-screen TV and a couple of ugly couches as well as a king-sized bed covered in a purple velvet bedspread and pushed into a corner of the back wall. My stomach turns just to look at it.

I feel like hurling. *God, give me composure. Please!* Whatever is about to transpire down here, I know that I have to pass this test.

Jimmy is sitting in a recliner with his eyes fixed on the TV screen. I'm relieved to see that he's only watching baseball. I don't know what I expected exactly, but everything about this house is so creepy and nasty and disgusting that I am continually bracing myself for the worst.

"So you got your shower?" he says without taking his eyes off the TV screen.

"Yeah." I try to sound cheerful. "Thanks. I really feel better."

"That's good. We want to take especially good care of you."

"Thanks," I say again.

"Sounds like we'll have you with us for a few more days," he tells me.

"How long?" Tatiana asks with irritation.

"As long as it takes," he snaps back at her.

She cusses now with a dark scowl, folding her arms across her front.

"Get over yourself," he says as he mutes the TV. Now he looks directly at me. "Tatiana is miffed because you're in her room and she's having to bunk with Kandy now."

"Oh?" I give Tatiana a sympathetic look. "I'm sorry to inconvenience you."

"Shut *up!*" She swears at me. "I've had enough of your Miss Congeniality act, Serena. You might be able to fool Ruby, but I'm not that stupid."

I give her an innocent look. "What do you mean?"

"I mean, *give it up*. We all know you want out of here. Don't try to act like you don't. We're not buying it." She glares at Jimmy. "At least I'm not. I can't speak for you."

"That's right." He stands up, coming over to check me out more closely. "You can't. And as long as we're getting our cut on this deal, we'll take good care of her, Tatiana. You get that?"

She scowls again.

"I'm really sorry that I put you out of your room. I'm willing to share a room with someone else if that helps."

"No," Jimmy says firmly. "You'll stay where you are."

"Until Mr. T," Tatiana says in a sneering tone. "After that, I'm taking it back."

"We'll see," Jimmy tells her.

"You mean you'll let me come back here *after* Mr. T?" I try to sound hopeful, like this is a place I want to return to.

"That depends." Jimmy is studying me closely now.

"On what?"

"On you."

"How so?" I'm carefully watching both of them, trying to read their expressions. Tatiana looks slightly worried, but Jimmy is more curious.

"Well, we just assumed that you wouldn't want to come back here. They usually don't."

"Why is that?" I ask.

Tatiana laughs. "Are you really that ignorant?"

"They don't usually want to come back because they never wanted to be here in the first place," Jimmy explains. "Just like you."

"How do you know that?" I lock gazes with him.

He shrugs. "We know you were brought here against your will."

"Really?" I tip my head to one side. "And who told you that?"

His brow creases. "I guess I just assumed it. That's usually the case."

"Well, maybe you should ask Marcia and Bryce. I'm sure they can tell you I put up no resistance. I mean, sure, I was surprised. I honestly thought I was going to get a modeling job." I laugh. "How naive was that?"

Tatiana snickers. "Well, at least you know better now."

"So after I got over myself," I continue, "I figured I should just make the best of it. I mean, it's not like I had anything to go back to anyway." I repeat the tale that I gave Ruby. I don't expect to get their pity, but I do hope they'll think I'm here willingly.

"Are you saying you want to be part of our little family?" Jimmy asks hopefully.

"Don't fall for her lies."

"Shut up, Tatiana," he snaps at her. "In fact, why don't you make yourself scarce. I'm getting sick of you."

She swears at him now, but then she leaves. And I have made a serious enemy. After the door slams, Jimmy sits back down in the recliner and invites me to sit on the couch. I'm surprised at how nice it feels to sit on something besides the floor and the bed.

"So tell me, Serena, how do you think you can fit in here?" Jimmy begins this conversation almost as if it's a job interview.

I'm caught off guard by how he seems too intelligent to be involved in a place like this. "What can you contribute to this household after your date with Mr. T?"

I let out a long sigh. "To be honest, it's all new to me, Jimmy. And I'm not really looking forward to Mr. T."

He laughs. "Yeah, well, I can understand that."

"But I realize that I need to cooperate. I know that a lot of money is involved. That Marcia and Bryce are invested in me. And it sounds like you are too."

"You got that right. There's a lot riding on this deal." He smiles. "I'm glad you understand that. Most of the girls we get here for Mr. T aren't that smart."

I nod. "Yeah, I've heard that most of them don't come back here."

"But you really think you want to?"

"I guess I'm curious what the alternative is. For some reason I've gotten the impression it's not that great."

He shakes his head in a sad way. "You got that right. Most of Mr. T's girls don't last too long. They're just not tough enough. I'm sorry to say a lot of them end up at the morgue."

I try to conceal my shock. "Because of Mr. T? Does he kill them?"

"No, no, nothing like that. It's because they didn't choose to be here in the first place, Serena. Because they resist and they fight back. And sometimes that causes them to get injured, you know?"

I nod, remembering the screaming from last night. "Yeah, I can understand that."

"And sometimes they take their own lives."

"Oh . . ." My stomach twists at the thought.

"And there's other risks." He shrugs. "But what can you do?"

I look directly at him, trying to appear calm. "I really appreciate your honesty, Jimmy. I mean, this is all pretty new to me."

"So now let me tell you about the brighter side." He grins. "Maybe I can entice you to consider becoming part of our family." He describes what could be considered a glamorous lifestyle of fancy clothes, expensive cars, good food, and a lot of male attention. "It's the world's oldest profession," he tells me finally. "And in some places it's legal."

I'm so over my head and sickened by all this, but somehow I need to make him believe I'm seriously considering this lifestyle. "Can I ask a question?"

"That's why I invited you down here. Ask away."

"I'm not saying I don't want to stay here—I mean, after Mr. T—but what would my alternatives be? Well, besides the morgue, which I find pretty unappealing."

He laughs. "Marcia and Bryce still own you, and they have the right to continue selling your time to the highest bidders. Except that the price will drop down the longer you're working for them."

"Right."

"The downside of remaining with them is that they will shuffle you around and you will never be treated like a human."

"So how would it be possible for me to stay here?" I ask hopefully. "I mean, if Marcia and Bryce still own me?"

He narrows his eyes. "First of all, we have to decide if you can be trusted."

"Trusted?"

"The girls here are dependable. They understand the rules . . . and respect them. I'm not convinced you're ready for that yet. Your first taste of freedom and you'd probably run home to Mommy."

I know I need to think fast. "But you just told me all the benefits of working here. A girl like me—well, I come from poverty. My mom could barely afford to support both of us and now she's losing her job. I guess you could say I'm pretty desperate." I wave my hand. "And this house is way nicer than where I used to live."

He nods smugly. "It's not a bad setup."

"So you'd consider letting me stay here?" I keep my voice even, trying to conceal the disgust churning inside of me. "That's possible?"

"It's possible. First we'd have to pay off your debts to Marcia and Bryce. And after that you'd work for us."

I control my expression and just nod. The idea of me owing anything to any of these people is so ridiculous I can hardly stand it.

"Tom, that's my boss, will negotiate a price for you. And I'm sure you won't come cheap. But it's an investment."

"Uh . . . right." I remember reading about the slave trade in history books, but I never really imagined it was still flourishing.

"Tom has big plans for this house. He wants only the best of the best living and working here." He flashes a smarmy smile. "And you are an exceptionally pretty girl, with just the kind of look a lot of our more-sophisticated clientele are looking for."

"Thank you." It takes all my self-control to hide my disgust.

"And Tom is quite impressed with your photos and he likes that you created a Facebook page. Very forward thinking. Although we'll have to change the name on it, of course."

"It sounds as if you've given this plenty of thought." My stomach turns to think of how I put that stupid portfolio together, how I posted it out there for the whole world to see. Like I was going to be famous. How naive could I be?

"We try to cover our bases." He stands up and reaches for my hand, pulling me to my feet. "And now I'd like to give you a quick tour." He heads for the stairs. "That way you can see for yourself that this is actually a pretty cool place. A lot better than we used to have."

As he leads the way upstairs, he explains how each girl usually has her own room. "Although sometimes, like now, some girls have to share. But most of the time they have their own space. The house has five bedrooms."

"Does that mean five girls live here?"

"Right now there are five, counting you. I have my own room. But if you decide to join us, I might move someone down to the basement."

As we walk through the great room again, I glance out the front window to see that this house is in a regular suburban neighborhood. In fact, judging by the attractive house across the street, it's a pretty nice neighborhood.

Jimmy continues explaining the setup as we go up the stairs to the second floor. He is so matter-of-fact about everything, like this is just a normal business or a respectable boardinghouse he helps to manage. He's telling me how the girls sometimes entertain their dates here at the house. It actually feels like he is recruiting me — or like he's already hired me for a job and this is my "orientation."

"But only if they know the guys well enough to trust their discretion," he says at the top of the stairs. "Otherwise they meet up with each other at our place downtown."

"Wow, you have a location downtown too?" I act impressed.

"Oh, yeah," he says with pride. "At least Tom has an account with the owner. But I wouldn't be surprised if he doesn't own the place before long. We're very enterprising and profitable." Now he even brags about how their organization takes credit cards for services rendered.

Everything in me wants to demand to know how — how is it possible that all this takes place and no one notices? No one questions this house with all its "security" bars? No neighbors are suspicious of this den of ill repute where men must come and go at all hours of the night? Doesn't anyone think it's a little odd? Or do people out there just close their eyes to these things? Does anyone care?

Jimmy knocks on the first door and then just opens it. So much for privacy. "Hey Desiree," he calls out. "You up yet?"

A pretty girl with long messy blonde curls sits up in a big four-poster bed, yawning sleepily. "What's the deal, Jimmy?"

"I want you to meet someone." He tugs me fully into her room. "This is Serena. She's considering joining us."

Desiree frowns. "You woke me up to tell me *that?*"

"Hey, it's after noon already. Time to rise and shine, Miss Dawn." He chuckles and winks at me. "Desiree Dawn never gets up before dawn."

I'm looking around the room, which is painted a peaceful shade of blue, and while it's not very big, it is fairly nicely furnished. Jimmy opens up her closet now. "As you can see, Desiree has a nice wardrobe."

She just lets out a loud groan and flops back down in bed, pulling the periwinkle blue bedding over her head as if we're not there.

"She came to us with nothing." Jimmy pulls a pretty pink shoe out of her shoe rack. "Now she has all this."

"Yeah, yeah," she mutters from her bed. "Keep it down, would you?"

Jimmy points out a few other things like her TV and DVD player and Xbox and selection of the latest games. "She's a video-game addict," he quietly tells me.

"There are worse addictions!" She pelts a pillow at him. "Now get out of here."

He just laughs as he leads me out. The next room belongs to Kandy Kane. Her walls are painted bright red and her bed has a red-and-white striped comforter with lots of candy-striped pillows. Even Kandy's hair resembles peppermint in that it's been bleached to platinum and striped with hot pink. I'm sure I will never look at a candy cane in the same way again.

But at least Kandy is wide awake and a lot friendlier than Desiree. "Hey Jimmy Boy. Is this the new girl?" She speaks with what sounds like a southern accent as she comes over to look more closely. "You are pretty enough, but kinda boring if you don't mind me saying so." She points to my outfit and chuckles. "Sorry about those pitiful threads I loaned you, but when Ruby asked for clothes, I wasn't so sure. I mean, I'd never even met you."

"Hey, I appreciate them," I tell her.

"I guess I could find something a little nicer, 'specially hearing how you'll be stickin' around a few more days."

She glances over to where Tatiana is sitting in a hot pink velvet chair by the window, glowering. "Not everyone is happy that you're still here." Kandy smiles at Jimmy. "But I don't mind having a little ol' roommate for a while. As long as it's not a permanent arrangement, you know?"

She runs her hand over Jimmy's collar. "You got something for me, sugar?"

"Not right now, Kandy."

She glares at him. *"When?"*

"Later. I'm giving Serena the tour at the moment. I want her to see that you girls have it pretty good here."

"As long as y'all give us what we need, Jimmy Boy." She turns to me with a smile. "Yeah, we do have it pretty good. Better'n before anyway. So, are you thinking of joining our little family?"

I smile. "Yeah, I am."

"Oh, sure," Tatiana growls. "I'll just bet you are."

I face her. "I really am sorry to have taken your room."

Tatiana swears at me, then turns back to the window.

Kandy laughs. "Well, her room sure ain't much, if you noticed. That's why she's the one who always gets to relocate when a visitor comes."

"My room looked just fine," Tatiana tells Kandy. "Before I had to take all my stuff out."

"Maybe it's fine for you, but it's sure not my cup of tea."

"It's minimalist," Tatiana retorts. "And a lot better than all this candy-striped garbage. I swear it makes me want to gag sometimes."

"Yeah, and being a minimalist is so handy. It makes it so much easier to boot you out of your room," Kandy teases. "Maybe you wanna rethink that strategy, huh?"

Tatiana turns away again, looking out the barred window with her arms tightly folded across her front. Although she seems to have the most hostility of the group, I think that might actually be a good sign. Maybe she is the most discontent of the bunch. Maybe she secretly wants out as badly as I do.

But even as I think this, I feel baffled. They all appear to have some freedom. As if they can come and go at will. But then I remember those bars and locks and am not so sure.

The last room up here is Ruby's, and to my surprise, it looks very much like a child's bedroom. There are stuffed animals everywhere, and the bedspread on the twin-sized bed is a juvenile animal print I would've thought she'd find too childish. And yet she seems perfectly comfortable and at home as she shows me around. She seems to be most proud of the bookshelf next to her bed.

"I love to read." She holds up the book that was facedown on her bed. "If you ever want to borrow something, feel free."

"I'd love to borrow a couple books." I eagerly examine the titles. "It would help to pass the time."

She makes some suggestions and I leave with three paperbacks under my arm. I cannot believe how excited I am to have something to do if I get locked in my barren room again.

"So, what do you think?" Jimmy asks when we're downstairs again.

"I'm pleasantly surprised," I lie. "I hope you'll consider letting me stay with you." Hoping my eyes don't betray me, I glance out the front window. "This neighborhood is way better than where I used to live. And this house is lots nicer too." I turn and smile. "What's not to like?"

He grins. "I was hoping you'd see it that way."

"Where's your room?" I ask and suddenly wish I hadn't. Except that I'm trying to get the lay of the land, hoping I can figure out a way to escape. There has to be one room or window or door that's not locked tight.

"It's right down here. Down the hall from yours. Want to see?"

I really don't, but I simply nod, pretending I'm interested, and soon I'm in a big master suite decorated in masculine shades of brown and gray and black. "Very nice," I say as I peek into the attached bath, which is cleaner than the one I showered in this morning. "And you're a pretty good housekeeper, too."

He nods. "Yeah, my clients expect that."

"Oh?" I try not to look surprised. "So you work too? Like the girls?"

"There are no free rides here. I mean, sure, I get some breaks and privileges because I manage the house. But Tom expects me to pay my dues. Just like he'll expect you to do . . . if you join us."

Now I notice some bags and paraphernalia on the bureau, and although I've never really been around illegal drugs before, I can tell that's what I'm seeing. "Well, I hope Tom decides I'm worth it." I quickly look away, trying to act like I observed nothing. "I hope he'll give me a chance."

"Oh, I think he will. He knows a good thing when he sees it. And he keeps telling me how he wants to have the most successful business in town. He's got a lot of houses now, but this one is by far his best. And by best, I mean he's got his most profitable workers here." He holds his head high like this is something to be proud of.

I'm feeling really sick to my stomach now. As well as light-headed. "I, uh, I don't feel too good," I say in a shaky voice.

"Have you had anything to eat?"

"Not for a while." I feel myself weaving and he takes me by the arm, leading me out into the main room where he helps me sit on one of the couches.

"Take some deep breaths and I'll get you some soda. You probably have low blood sugar."

I lean over, feeling the blood rushing to my head and hoping I'm not about to throw up. But suddenly I'm so overwhelmed by all this. So saddened and sickened. How can all these young people act so nonchalant and complacent? They all act perfectly normal, as if there's nothing wrong with living like this. How is that even possible?

"Here you go," he says gently as he hands me a can of Sprite. "Drink up."

I gladly drink the cold soda, and whether it's the unexpected kindness or the sugar, I almost immediately feel better. "Thank you."

"Hasn't Tatiana been taking care of you?" He frowns. "Giving you food and stuff?"

I shrug. "She gave me a box of cereal and a jug of water the other day, and I've been trying to make it last. Also some pizza and a McMuffin a few days ago."

He swears now. "Tatiana is really pushing me lately. I need to talk to that girl."

"She's upset that I took her room. You shouldn't be too hard on her."

He studies me. "Are you really as nice as you seem? Or is Tatiana right? Are you just taking us all for a big fat ride?"

I look directly at him. "I'm sorry, but I just happen to really care about people. I care about you, and I care about Ruby, and even though she hates me, I care about Tatiana. I expect that I'll care about Kandy and Desiree too . . . once I get to know them. Is there something wrong with that?"

He gives a reassuring smile. "No. Not at all. I think Tom's gonna like you a lot, Serena."

Then Jimmy asks me what my favorite pizza is and, although I haven't liked Hawaiian since I was a kid, I ask for pineapple and ham. I listen as he calls out for delivery. Now I am literally salivating as I wait for the fresh, hot food to arrive.

Even though my plan to make friends seems to be working, and I can tell that Jimmy is slowly buying into my charade,

I still feel sickened and compromised just the same. Yet what can I do differently? It honestly feels like the only way to survive and eventually escape this hellhole is to play along and wait for the big moment when I can make my getaway. I just have no idea exactly how and when I will pull it off. But I am studying everything and everyone, trying to come up with a viable plan.

I'm relieved to see that Jimmy didn't order only one pizza. And when he yells up the stairs, inviting the others to come down for food, I'm actually excited to see everyone trek down. And just like that—almost like we really are a family—we're all sitting around the dining room table, pigging out on pizza.

Desiree is still in her nightie, but everyone else is dressed fairly normal. And really, if someone looked in on us just now, they wouldn't suspect anything out of the norm was going on in this house. For a moment, I wonder if I haven't just imagined everything.

But then Jimmy is looking at his iPhone and suddenly he's telling the girls the plans for the evening. "Kandy, Desiree, and Tatiana are invited to a private party at the Birmingham Inn." They seem happy to hear this. Although Tatiana, as usual, is scowling. Again, this gives me hope.

"What about me?" Ruby asks. "Wasn't I invited to the party?"

"You and me will go downtown together," he tells her.

She just nods, looking sadly down at her pizza.

That's when it all feels real again. Painfully real. I almost lose my appetite, but then remember that if I'm going to escape, I will need my strength. And if they're all going out tonight, it might be my big chance. My plan is to remain on my best behavior and to quietly retire to my room to read and hope I'm forgotten and no one shows up to dead-bolt me in.

I have no doubts that the house will be in lockdown, but I also feel like there should be a way out. And at the very least, I will break out a front window and start screaming for help from across the street.

It's weird how much improved my life feels with this new freedom to wander around the spacious house. It's exhilarating.
And I can almost imagine how a girl could get sucked into this
degenerate lifestyle — especially if she'd been locked up or barely
surviving on the streets. Although I know about Ruby, I'm curious to hear the other girls' stories and what possible reasons they
might have for being a willing part of this.

At the same time, it's tempting to try to hide from everything. I could just lose myself in the books Ruby loaned me, and
I'm sure they'll be a comfort at night when I'm locked back in
my room, if that happens. But in the meantime, the only way
I'll get out of here is to figure it out myself.

I remain in the kitchen after we're finished with the pizza.
My goal is to clean up in here and try to think of a way out. At
the very least I could use something heavy, like a pan, and bash
out the front window and scream for help. But only if I saw a
neighbor outside. So far, although I've noticed a few cars, I
haven't seen a single person out there.

It's weird, though, as badly as I want out of this creepy
place, I'd like to help these girls, too. I know they're trying to
act like they're okay with this disgusting lifestyle, but I can tell

they're not happy. And Ruby . . . she's so young. It's all so disturbing.

As I'm scrubbing the grubby granite countertop, I know I can't just escape and forget all about them. So I feel like I'm a spy, like I need to gather their stories without letting them discover my reasons for wanting to know. They would clam up if they knew my real motives.

"You don't have to do that," Kandy tells me as I'm loading the dishwasher with dishes that seem to have been sitting out for days. "We have a cleaning lady who comes on Monday mornings. She'll take care of everything."

"That's okay," I say as I tear off a paper towel. "I want to." I squirt some cleaner on the microwave, wiping off the grimy glass surface. "This is such a pretty kitchen. I've never been in a house this nice before. It's kind of fun to clean it."

"Seriously?" She frowns at me like I'm some sort of anomaly, then reaches for one of the liquor bottles. She finds a clean glass and fills it with something amber. Then, after taking a long swig, she lets out a deep sigh. "Ahh . . . just what the doctor ordered." She takes another long gulp. "At least until Jimmy gets me what I *really* need."

She empties the glass, then clanks it down on the counter with a bang, swearing. "Sometimes that lazy dude makes me really want to scream and pull my hair out." She looks around. "Where is he anyway?"

"I don't know." I continue scrubbing something sticky from the stove top.

She leans over, peering curiously at me. "What are you doing here anyway? What's your game, *Pollyanna*?"

"Pollyanna?"

She nods. "Yeah, that's what you remind me of. The girl

who's trying to pretend this is a good place to be. Like you're playing the glad game."

I look back evenly at her. "I'm just trying to get by. No different than you. Surviving the best way I can."

She laughs and I'm reminded of Michelle's sometimes-sarcastic laugh. "Yeah, right. You're just like me. Well, excuse me for sayin' so, but you don't look like no junkie to me."

"Is that how you do this?"

She slaps her palm on the counter so loudly it makes me jump. "It is *why* I do this," she seethes at me. "Don't you get that?"

I slowly nod, stunned at how Kandy can be sweeter than sugar one minute and meaner than the devil the next. Probably the drugs. "Yeah, I get it. You do what you do to get what you need."

"You got that right, Pollyanna." She yells for Jimmy now, and without saying another word to me, she goes off in search of him, eventually pounding on his bedroom door and yelling for him to answer.

After several minutes, he opens it and she goes inside and the whole time I'm cleaning the kitchen, she doesn't come back out. A chill runs through me as I realize that they're probably both getting high in there together. Who else in this house depends on drugs to get by?

I'm just finishing in the kitchen, which looks impressive if I do say so myself, when Ruby comes back. She's digging through the fridge, which I discovered was mostly empty except for sodas and a few random condiments, a jar of olives, and some nasty-smelling lunch meat, which I threw out.

"The housekeeper will be here tomorrow." Ruby pops open a Mountain Dew, pouring it into a glass with ice.

"So I've heard." I return the broom to the closet where I found it. "I just felt like doing this. *Okay?*"

She nods with a slightly apologetic expression. "Sure . . . yeah . . . okay."

I give a partial smile. "Sorry to be so grouchy. I guess I'm just trying to figure stuff out."

"What kind of stuff?"

"Oh, you know, what keeps you guys all going. I know that Kandy and Jimmy rely on drugs." I tip my head toward the hallway.

"Yeah. Desiree and Tatiana do too. Except they mostly smoke weed. Kandy and Jimmy are into the hard stuff. I tried it, but it made me so sick I decided never again. And Jimmy respects that." She reaches for a bottle of vodka, pouring a generous portion into her greenish yellow soda.

"You really like *that*?" As usual, I try to conceal my shock. For some reason I had assumed that Ruby, maybe because of her juvenile room or her age, was the one who might not be abusing a substance.

She takes a sip and wrinkles her nose. "It helps to numb me." She points to the clock on the microwave and I see that it's already past five. "I usually start drinking around this time of day. That way I'm feeling good by the time we're out there, you know, drumming up business." She makes a sad little laugh and takes another big sip.

"What if you could get out of this life?" I ask quietly. "Would you want to?"

She rolls her eyes. "Yeah, and I'd want a million dollars, too. Are you the good fairy, handing out wishes?"

I shrug. "Just curious. Like I said, I'm trying to figure this stuff out."

She studies me. "Some people don't have a choice. We just take what we get, and like I said, we hope things'll get better . . . someday."

"What if you were out working, I mean, like you'll be doing tonight," I persist, "and what if someone came along and promised to take you away from all this? Would you go?"

She laughs. "Sure. That happens all the time. Every guy has a line."

"Not like that. What if someone wanted to rescue you?"

She frowns. "You better watch what you say, Serena. I like you, but you could get in trouble talking like that. Tom has friends everywhere. No one can run away from him. Not and live to talk about it."

"What about the police?" I whisper.

She scowls. "Okay, that just shows how totally ignorant you really are."

"What do you mean?"

"The last girl who talked to the police was returned in a bloody heap. That happened just before I came here. Britney was my best friend in the other house. But her face was so messed up that she couldn't work anymore. Jimmy had to let her go."

"Free?"

"No." She shakes her head and lowers her voice. "No one goes free. The sooner you get that, the better. I don't know what happened to Britney, but I know it wasn't good." She finishes off her drink and starts to mix another. "I'm not the smartest thing around, but I do know better than to run to the police."

Someone is coming down the stairs. As Tatiana enters the room, Ruby is rattling on about her favorite reality shows. "I told Jimmy we should do a reality show here," she says lightly. I can tell the alcohol is already taking effect.

"Here in this house?" I ask in disbelief.

"Yeah, don't you think it'd be a good show?" she asks me. "Desperate Runaways of the Great Northwest. We could have cameras in every room."

Tatiana lets out a laugh. "That's not a bad idea, Ruby."

"Yeah, I know." Ruby takes her drink over to where Tatiana is now cruising through the TV channels. "Don't you think people would be interested in knowing how the other half lives?"

"For sure." Tatiana nods. "We could all get rich and famous."

"Except that Tom would never allow it." Ruby flops down on a sofa.

Tatiana is clicking away on the remote and, to my surprise, she stops on the TV Land channel and *The Andy Griffith Show* is just starting.

I sit on the couch next to Ruby, and the three of us quietly watch as Aunt Bee tells Opie how important it is to honor his word and keep his promises. Incongruous, yes? But it feels even stranger when Tatiana lights up a joint and starts puffing. I can't help but cough and, excusing myself, I slowly stand.

Tatiana just laughs at me. "Yeah, I figured that would get rid of you."

"Sorry," I say as I wave the air. "But I'm actually pretty tired."

"Yeah, well, enjoy my room," she says bitterly.

As I go into her barren room, I wonder what there is to enjoy. But I close the door, still hoping they'll all forget about locking me up when they leave tonight. I open one of Ruby's paperbacks and get lost in a happy story for a while. Eventually, I hear someone at my door and the familiar clank of the dead bolt as it is snapped into place.

"Wait!" I leap up to pound on the door. "I still need to use the bathroom and fill my water bottle first."

"Should've thought of that earlier," Tatiana says dully.

I call out to her, pleading with her to come back and give me a second chance, but as I press my ear to the door, I can only hear the sound of girls' voices and eventually the bang of what must be the front door slamming. After that it's just silence.

It's obvious no one here really cares about me. How could I expect them to? Especially when their own lives are so messed up — everything is pretty much out of their control too. As I go back to the mattress, I suppress my tears. I have to toughen up. And smarten up. But as I pick up my book, I'm somewhat amazed that those people in their various inebriated states could still remember to lock me up in here. I wouldn't have thought they'd be that functional.

As I look around the room, I wish I'd thought to sneak one of the pans from the kitchen, something I could use to break this window. Now that I know this house is in a somewhat normal neighborhood, I am ready to give that a try. But maybe I should pace myself since that's not exactly a foolproof idea.

What I really want to do is find myself sort of alone in the house. Like I almost was while cleaning the kitchen this afternoon. And then, God willing and with his help, I will break out of this prison. And I'll do what I can to help the others. If they'll allow themselves to be helped.

It's not until Tuesday that I'm let out of my cage again. It's very hard to keep up my act, pretending like all this is okay. And yet it's the only way to win their trust. And for some reason—a reason that's nearly escaped me at the moment—this still seems important.

"There's some food in the kitchen," Tatiana blandly informs me as she walks away.

I mumble a quiet thank-you and go into the bathroom, which has actually been cleaned, and there I gulp down some water and then take a shower. I'm not sure if it's my imagination or the nasty mattress I've been sleeping on, but I'm all itchy and rashy now, like something has been biting me.

After I shower, I put on my little black dress—only because it's cleaner than the shorts and T-shirt I've been wearing 24/7. And I put my damp hair into a ponytail. Then I go out to search for food. The whole house seems tidier, then I remember that someone was supposed to come in to clean on Monday morning.

I open the fridge to see there is some food, and I wonder who provided it. Maybe the cleaning lady. Anyway, I eat some peach yogurt and some orange juice and a banana and begin to feel almost human again.

"There you are," Jimmy says. "Just the girl I'm looking for."

I give him a slightly blank look as I drop the banana peel and yogurt container into the trash. I know I should be handling myself and my emotions better, but I'm so exhausted.

"Marcia just gave me a message for you." He waves a piece of paper in front of me like a flag.

"What's that?" Suddenly I'm hoping for the impossible — that Marcia has come to her senses and decided to set me free.

"Marcia wants you to know that *so far* everyone is okay." He examines the paper. "She says not to worry and that Ginnie Fremont is just fine."

I try not to look surprised that they know my mom's first name.

"And Michelle Diedericks and Trista and Leo and Lacy Burk are all fine too." He gives me a questioning look.

But I just shrug. "Why wouldn't they be?"

He slowly smiles. "Exactly. That's just what I told Marcia. You've given no reason for anyone to retaliate against anyone. And I'm sure that's how it will continue to go."

I can't show him how disturbing it is to hear everyone's full names and this not-so-veiled threat just as I'm plotting to escape from here. I'm sure that's why Marcia gave him that information. Just to keep me in my place. And although part of me questions whether or not Marcia and her goons would actually carry out their evil threats, I know I have to go about this very carefully now. These people are not to be taken lightly. And they want me to know it.

Instead of reacting, I hold out my bare arm, showing Jimmy the red spots I've gotten. "I don't think Mr. T is going to like seeing me looking all rashy like this. Do you think there's something wrong with the bed?"

He actually looks slightly concerned. "Maybe so. I'll make a call to Tom, tell him we need a new mattress."

"Thanks."

"If we knew you were staying, I'd let you take over Tatiana's room and fix it up." He peers curiously at me.

"But where would Tatiana stay?"

"Maybe the basement." He shrugs. "We'll see."

Imagining Tatiana imprisoned in the dank basement makes me cringe. Not only for her sake but mine, since I'm sure she'd take it out on me. "Or maybe she and I could share a room."

"Seriously?" He frowns. "You'd *want* to share a room with Tatiana?"

"Sure. Why not?" It's possible that Tatiana is the one who wants out of here the most. She seems to wear her anger on her sleeve, and I can't help but think she's got the brains and the guts to make a break. Especially if she had some encouragement. "It just seems fair . . . I mean, since it was her room first."

"Well, I'll give that some thought. In the meantime, you go talk to Desiree about something to clear up that skin. Tatiana is who you go to for hair, but Desiree is the real beauty expert around here. She'll probably have some lotion or cream to get rid of that rash."

I find Desiree just coming out of the bathroom upstairs. Wearing a silky black robe and her hair in a towel, she is not particularly pleased to see me. And even though I explain that Jimmy sent me to her, she doesn't seem inclined to help me. "Come back later."

"I could do that." I follow her into her room, ignoring the brush-off. "Or maybe I could just borrow something now."

"What*ever*." Her voice drips with irritation.

"Sorry to be a pest." I go to her bureau, which is loaded with lotions and cosmetics. "Wow." I act impressed. "You know what to do with all this stuff?"

"Of course." Desiree flops down on a chair and begins to towel-dry her hair.

"I've never been good with this kind of thing," I admit honestly.

"It's not that hard. You take care of your skin and it'll take care of you."

"Really?" I pick up a jar of cream. "How did you learn that?"

"My grandma." She sighs as she starts pulling a brush through her hair. "She was the only one in my life who cared about me."

"What happened to her?" I ask as I open a jar and smell.

"She got cancer and died. *Okay?*" Desiree tosses down her hairbrush and frowns. "Just take the aloe vera, would you? And beat it."

"Which one is it?"

She jumps up now, grabs a green bottle, and thrusts it at me. "Here!" She's on the verge of tears, and I don't want to lose this moment.

"My grandma died about five years ago," I tell her. This is actually true. "I kinda know how you feel." Okay, this is not so true. I was never close to my grandma. She lived on the East Coast, and she and Mom didn't really get along. "I'm sorry."

"Yeah, well, that's life, isn't it?"

"I guess so." I squirt some of the aloe vera into my palm. Stalling, I rub it onto the rash. "Didn't you have any other family?"

"Not really. My dad died of a drug overdose so long ago I can't even remember him. And my mom's been in prison for dealing since I was about six. Grandma was all I had. After she was gone, I landed in foster care." She picks up her hairbrush again. "And that pretty much sucked."

"Yeah . . . I can imagine."

She narrows her eyes. "Really? Can you?"

I nod earnestly. "Yeah. There were some foster families in the apartment complex where I lived. Didn't seem like real happy places. I figure they take in the kids just for the money."

"Well, you got that one right."

I want to add that not all of the foster families were bad, but since she seems to be softening, I hold my tongue. "So you decided to join up with Tom then?" I wipe some lotion on the other arm.

"Decided?" She laughs without humor. "Yeah, right."

I pretend to focus on getting the aloe vera spread evenly. And it's actually fairly soothing on the broken-out patches.

"No one really decides to join up with Tom."

I nod, putting some lotion on my legs now.

"I met Jimmy on the streets and he helped me out of a bad situation. He got me a place to live and some clothes and food. He took care of me."

This sounds familiar. Jimmy finds an attractive girl who's down on her luck and wins her over with stuff. Most likely it's stuff financed by Tom. Once the girl feels indebted to him, they tighten the net and pull her in.

"So what if you wanted to leave now?" I ask absently, not looking up as I smooth the lotion over my other leg.

She releases that sarcastic laugh again.

I stand up straight, just looking at her. "So if you want to walk away and start a new life . . . you can't?"

She glances toward her still-open door and frowns.

"I'm just curious. Trying to figure things out for myself. Jimmy is offering to let me stay here."

"There are worse places. Believe me, I know."

"But what about freedom?" I say quietly. "Or rights?"

She turns away with a stony look.

"Just because Jimmy was kind to you doesn't mean you owe him. It's wrong to be held against your will and you—"

"Shut up!" she hisses at me. "You don't have any idea what you're talking about . . . or who you're dealing with."

"I'm just saying—"

"I'm saying to shut up!" she shouts.

"Sorry, I—"

"Talk to me a year from now!" she growls. "That is, if you're still around. Then you can tell me all about freedom and rights." She points to the door. "For now, you can get out!"

Despite her hostility toward me, I feel somewhat hopeful as I replace the aloe vera lotion on the bureau.

"Just take it with you," she barks at me. "And get the **** out!"

I hurriedly thank her and, grabbing up the lotion, make a fast exit. I must've triggered something to get such a strong response from her. Hopefully our conversation, no matter how painful, will get her to think.

"What's wrong with Desiree?" Ruby asks as we meet at the top of the stairs.

I shrug. "Guess I hit a nerve."

Ruby frowns. "Seems like everyone's in a bad mood today."

"Why's that?"

"Kandy's holed up in her room." She rolls her eyes. "Probably coming down from last night. But then Tatiana and Jimmy just had a big fight downstairs. She sounds really, really mad."

"I hope it's not because of me."

"Why would it be?"

I tell Ruby about Jimmy's idea to move Tatiana to the basement.

"Uh-oh . . ." Ruby shakes her head. "That's not good."

"Yeah. And I told him I wouldn't mind sharing a room with her."

Ruby makes a grim expression. "The only one who can stand Tatiana for long is Kandy, and that's because she's so strung out most of the time."

"Well, thanks for the heads-up."

"You could always share my room with me," she offers. "I wouldn't mind. Maybe we could put another bed in there."

"That'd be cool with me. Why don't you mention it to Jimmy? Might be better coming from you."

"Okay. But I'll wait for him to cool off. He and Tatiana were really going at it. I was afraid it was going to turn into a real knock-down, drag-out fight. Ya know?"

I grimace. "Yeah, I know."

Feeling a bit like a troublemaker and then wondering why, I fill up my water bottle and even grab some provisions from the kitchen—just in case I get stuck in lockdown again, which seems fairly likely considering how many times Tatiana has locked me up in there and then forgotten to let me out.

Included in my stash is a large jar of salsa that might be useful as a projectile. I'm hoping that the solid-feeling jar is strong enough to break the bedroom window if I hurl it hard enough. And I'm just starting to feel desperate enough to do that—if no one is home to hear it, that is.

It's getting late in the afternoon, but seeing that I still have some freedom, I take my dirty bedding and the spare clothes from Kandy to the laundry room, where I put them in the washer and turn it on. While I'm there, I spot some clean sheets and a fuzzy green blanket in a plastic laundry basket.

Feeling extraordinarily fortunate, I carry these back to my room where I've already layered some towels from the bathroom onto the mattress, which I'm sure must be filled with bedbugs. As I attempt to improve this sorry bed, I hope Jimmy comes through with a new one before long. However, I'm not holding my breath. And once it's neatly made, I tuck the salsa underneath the pillow. Just in case someone drops by and wonders, not that I've had many visitors of late.

I'm really praying for God to make a way out of here for me. I haven't heard anyone talking about working tonight, but as far as I can tell, every night is a working night in this place. And if they are going out tonight, I'm hoping that with Tatiana out of sorts with Jimmy, she'll forget to lock my door before they leave. Really, it seems like she, even more than the rest, has the most to gain if I get out of here. She should be happy to have me disappear while everyone is out. How convenient for her — she'll get her room back. And this horrid mattress, too.

I do wish that I could rescue everyone in this place, but as the minutes and hours and days just keep on ticking by, pushing me closer and closer to the inevitable date with Mr. T, I figure I better focus on getting myself out. Before it's too late. Now if only God would help me to escape.

CHAPTER 13

"I see you're already making yourself at home here," Tatiana says as she walks into my room. I hate that I actually consider this my room, but sadly it's true. She leans over to pick up the edge of the fuzzy green blanket, and giving it a hard pull, she jerks it off. "But that's mine." Now she does the same with the sheets. "So are these." Of course, the jar of salsa rolls out, tumbling onto the floor. "And what is this?" She picks it up.

"Midnight snack?" I say a bit glibly.

She narrows her eyes as she tosses it in the air, catching it with one hand. Then bouncing the jar in her hand, she stares at the window as if she knows exactly what I planned to do with it.

"Look," I say quickly. "I *know* this is your room. And I don't even want to be in it. I'd gladly give it back to you if I could. And Ruby has offered to let me stay with her. I would've told Jimmy already, but I haven't seen him." I wave my hand. "But believe me, I'd happily evacuate for you — if I could."

She glares at me. "Yeah, I bet you would. Now that you've infected my mattress with your lice and bedbugs."

Everything in me wants to rise up and lash out at her now. How dare she accuse me of infecting her nasty old bed! But I suspect she wants to get a reaction out of me. She'd probably like an excuse to lay into me. And judging by the look in her eye, she'd probably mess me up pretty badly. But instead of reacting, I pray for God to give me the right words.

"I just want out of here," I quietly confess to her. "I want to be free again . . . to come and go and live my life as I please. And I think you want the same thing."

"You don't know me well enough to know what I want," she snarls. "Don't pretend like you do."

"Fine. I'm just being honest with you." I look down at my bare feet. "Sorry I took your blanket and sheets. I didn't realize they were yours. You can have them back—"

"Don't worry," she says lightly. "I will. I'll have it all back."

I look up, locking gazes with her.

"In a few days this room will be mine again."

"Oh . . . ?"

"Yeah, I heard Jimmy talking to Tom earlier. Your big date is set for Friday night. Sounds like Mr. T came through with the big bucks. His expectations are probably really high. You should be preparing yourself, Serena. I'm sure it'll be a night you'll never forget."

She laughs meanly, but her eyes look slightly concerned. That is, unless I'm imagining things.

"So come Friday, you'll be on your merry little way."

"What if I want to come back?"

She looks at the jar of salsa in her hand and then shakes her head. "No, I think I was right about you all along. After your date with Mr. T, you'll probably fall apart. Or you'll try to run away. Or kill yourself." She shrugs like it makes no difference. "That's how it usually goes down."

Now the room is silent, and feeling like I'm on the verge of tears, I turn away and pretend to be looking out the window.

How can a person—especially someone who's stuck in the same dead-end lifestyle—be so emotionally disconnected and hateful? How can she be so cruel and heartless?

"I know what you're thinking," she says quietly. I'm actually surprised that she's still here. But maybe she just wants to torment me some more.

I turn around and just gaze at her. "What am I thinking?" I ask in a weary tone. I feel so tired . . . so exhausted . . . so beaten.

"You can't believe I'm such a witch. You think I should become your pal and help you to get out of here. You think I should want out of here too. Right?"

I bite into my lip. No matter how I answer this, it will come out wrong.

"Well, you haven't seen the things I've seen, Serena. You haven't experienced what I've experienced. You don't know what you don't know."

I look directly into her eyes. "I know that this is wrong. I know that Tom is treating everyone in this house like slaves. He's using all of you for his own gain. He doesn't care about any of you."

"Tell me something I don't know, Serena."

"How can you live with that?" I quietly demand. "Don't you think you're worth more than that?"

She gives me a disgusted look. "Worth more? Meaning that Tom should charge more for me?"

"No. I mean as a person. Don't you think you're worth more than settling for a life like this—a life of slavery?"

"What if this is all there is? What if a girl like me will never have more than this? Besides"—she glances over her shoulder—"no one ever gets away. Not really. She gets caught and beaten and then shuffled to different places, worse places. But no one gets away. Well, unless she dies."

"I'm going to get away. I know God is preparing a way of escape for me."

She laughs. "Well, I can't wait to see how that turns out."

"You could get away too," I say hopefully. "We could help each other."

She looks bored now. "Even if we got out, we wouldn't get far. I don't know why you can't get that through your head. Tom has people everywhere. As soon as you think you can trust someone, you find out that she's working for Tom or one of his friends."

"God is bigger than Tom."

She tosses the blanket and sheets back on the bed. "You might as well use these for now," she says bitterly. "You'll be gone soon enough. And talking like you do, I'm pretty certain you won't be back." She gives me a sad smile. "Hopefully they won't be carrying you out in a body bag, though. I almost think I could've learned to like you." Now with the salsa still in her hand, she goes out and I hear the dead bolt being locked . . . once again.

It's about an hour before I hear the sounds of them leaving. I can't tell if everyone is gone or not, but the house is so quiet, I figure they're all out. I look at the window. Would I have had the nerve to pelt the jar of salsa through it? It would've taken a good, hard throw. And then I would've had to be ready to scream my head off until someone heard me. And what if no one did? Then I'd have to explain the broken glass and salsa mess to Jimmy.

I suppose I could've claimed temporary insanity. Although I suspect he'd reward me with a zap from his little stun gun. And it would probably hurt. But would it be any worse than this? Counting the days until Mr. T?

I haven't given up on God—and I don't plan to—but I honestly don't know why this is taking so long. I don't know how far it will go. And I'm not even sure I can keep myself together during the next four days.

As I pray myself to sleep, just like I do every night, I ask God to help me connect with every single person in this house. And I pray for God to release them from this evil prison where they are being deceived and abused and used by people with no regard for human rights or freedom.

"Please, show them that you can deliver anyone from anything," I plead with God. "Show them that you have a better life . . . if only they'd be willing. Open their eyes. Help them to see that you can do anything . . . for anyone."

As I'm praying, I get a strong sense that God wants me to become more outspoken—for him. And I decide that for the next few days, probably my last days in this place, I will become bold. With God's help, I'll try to be his mouthpiece and tell everyone here that God has a plan for their lives. Who knows, they might respond . . . or they might get so sick of me that they throw me out. Here's hoping.

I'm not surprised that the sun's high in the sky before my door opens the next day. Tatiana looks a little worse for wear, and she smells like BO and stale marijuana smoke.

"Thank you," I say brightly. "And God bless you." I hurry to the bathroom, thankful that I made it long enough to avoid using the detestable bucket in the closet. I've never been so thankful for something as basic as indoor plumbing.

"God bless *me*?" Tatiana says as she follows me to the bathroom. Never mind privacy. She just stands there waiting by the sink as I relieve myself.

"Yes." I flush the toilet. "I've been praying for God to bless you."

"Right . . ." She just shakes her head. "You're obviously losing it, Serena. Sorry about that. It happens to the best and the worst of us."

"No, I'm fine," I assure her as I wash my hands. "It's just that I realize you're probably right. I might not get to come back here after Friday. And I want to be sure to tell everyone in this house about how much God loves them before I go." I smile as I dry my hands. "Starting with you."

"Uh-huh." Her face is pure skepticism. "God loves me? Yep, I can sure feel that love. It's just oozing all over my life." She points at me. "And you too, huh? If this is how God loves people, I'd hate to be on his hate list."

"It might interest you to know that the disciples, the guys who were Jesus' best friends, all ended up being imprisoned and eventually killed for their faith. But they never gave up believing in him. Just because a person has problems doesn't mean that God quit loving them."

She looks slightly interested. "What *does* it mean then?"

"It means that God allows hard stuff into our lives because he wants to remind us to call out to him for help. He wants us to know that we need him. And then he can deliver us and be glorified."

"And how exactly is that working for you?"

I hold up my hands. "Hey, I'm not saying I have all the answers. But I figure if I keep on trusting God . . . if I keep waiting on him . . . in time he's going to make a way for me to escape."

"But what about those disciples who went to prison or got killed? How did they escape?"

I consider this. "They had an eternal escape. They're in heaven with him right now. Probably having a great time. Life isn't just here on earth. Eternity is forever."

She looks doubtful.

"Because you gotta admit, we're all going to die someday," I press on with my sermonette, thankful that she's still listening. "For some, it's going to end sooner than later. All the more reason to start trusting God right now." I point at her. "For instance, what if you died tonight?"

She rolls her eyes. "What if I did?"

"Where would you go?"

"To the morgue." She's peering in the mirror now, frowning at her pale, pinched face. Can she see how sad and pathetic she looks? Does she have any idea where her life is headed?

"And after the morgue? Where would your spirit go?"

She frowns. "I guess I'll find out when I get there, won't I?"

"But don't you want your spirit to be with God?" I stare into her eyes, which are staring into the mirror with a really blank expression. "After all the hell you've been through on this earth, Tatiana? Don't you long for something more? Something better? Something to hope for? I mean, besides the morgue and being buried six feet under?"

She lets out a tired sigh, turning away from the mirror. "Sure, it'd be great. Except that all that heaven crud is just a fairy tale. And I quit believing in fairy tales after the world kicked me in the teeth a few times." She leaves the bathroom and I follow her into the great room.

"Millions of people, probably billions even, believe that God is real, Tatiana. They don't think heaven is a fairy tale. And I believe he's real too."

"Well, good for you, Serena. I'll be curious to see how your beliefs help you when you get handed over to Mr. T this week."

I know she's trying to make me squirm, but I'm determined to stand firm. "God will take care of me," I say boldly, and at the same time I'm inwardly praying that God won't hang me out to dry on this. "I will never stop trusting him."

She gives me a dubious look, then pauses to peer out the front window. "What is *that*?" She moves closer to investigate. I follow and we both stand there watching as a moving truck slowly backs into the driveway of this house.

"Maybe that's my new bed," I say optimistically.

She gives me a withering look, then turns back to the window.

"Is that our hot tub?" Kandy says as she joins us. "Jimmy said we're getting one before winter." She yells over her shoulder. "Hey, Jimmy. Come see if this is our hot tub."

Jimmy wanders out of his bedroom with a sleepy look. "Huh? What's up?"

"Look." Tatiana points. "There's a truck in the driveway. It says Willamette Freight Line on the side. Maybe you should check—"

"What the—" And like a shot, Jimmy dashes past us and into the laundry room where he's fiddling with keys and unlocking the door, which I assume must lead out to the garage. All the time he's swearing up a storm, and we all cluster in the laundry room to see what he's so upset about.

"This was not supposed to happen again," he says as the garage door opens. "Tom promised."

Seeing daylight as the door rises, I'm tempted to make a run for it, but Tatiana and Kandy are standing in front of me, and all I can do is just watch over their shoulders as the truck backs right up to the opening. And then a skinny guy comes around and slides up the rolling door on the truck, and suddenly a bunch of people pour out.

It's all women and children. And mostly they appear to be Asian or Hispanic. They're barely out of the truck when the garage door is lowered and the daylight is blocked out. A large guy is walking toward us now, smiling like there's nothing the least bit strange about this delivery.

"No, no, no." Jimmy holds his hands up. "You cannot bring them in here, Mitch. No way."

"You tell that to the boss man." This Mitch dude is about a head taller and maybe twice Jimmy's weight, and he doesn't seem to care what Jimmy thinks. He and two other guys are herding the women and children away from the garage door, pushing them toward the laundry room like sheep.

Jimmy's face is red now. "But Tom promised—"

"Tom's the one who sent them here!" Mitch snaps at Jimmy. "Now get 'em out of this garage fast. Tom said to keep them in the basement for the time being."

"But that's not fair."

Mitch raises a fist at Jimmy. "You telling me what is and ain't fair, little man?"

"But Tom said—" And just like that, Mitch smacks Jimmy right in the face. Jimmy stumbles backward, and Kandy jumps down into the garage to help catch him.

"Get outta the way," Mitch yells at us girls. "Let these people in right now before anyone else gets hurt."

We all back up into the house and into the kitchen, watching as what looks like about twenty or so people flood through the laundry room and into the house. They look as confused and frightened as I feel. They all huddle together in the great room as if they're afraid to move or speak.

"Come on." Tatiana waves at the crowd of newcomers. "To the basement, all of you."

"That's right!" Mitch yells. "At least Tatiana knows how to follow orders. Maybe we ought to put her in charge of this place."

Tatiana lets out some colorful language as she herds the women and children toward the door that leads to the basement. Amazingly, no one questions her authority over them. They simply file toward the door and obediently head down the stairs, where for all they know they could be going into a gas chamber — like what I've read happened in Auschwitz. They all seem skinny and dirty and are dressed in little more than rags.

Eventually the last of them goes down the stairs, and then Tatiana closes the door and bolts it securely. "There."

Mitch has Jimmy by the shoulder now, glaring down at him. "Are you gonna question Tom about this, or are you gonna follow orders?"

Jimmy's nose is bleeding and his lower lip is starting to swell. "But Tom said — "

"Tom said for me to let my fists do the talking," he yells into Jimmy's face. "You really want more?"

Jimmy shakes his head. "What are we supposed to do with them?" he asks meekly.

"Keep 'em here until Tom finds a new place for them. It's not like we could keep them in the truck. It's ninety degrees outside. They would be baked to a crisp."

"How long will we have them?"

"How am I supposed to know? You must've heard that the place on the east side was gonna get busted. And Tom's pretty sure the house in Mallard Park is under surveillance. For all I know, we might have to bring those kids here too. Just until we find the next place or new owners."

"But you can't bring everyone here," Jimmy protests.

Mitch gives him a threatening look and a hard shake. "This is Tom's business, Jimmy. Not yours. You, my little man, are replaceable. You better not forget it." Then he releases him so hard that Jimmy falls onto the kitchen floor, hitting his forehead on the corner of a cabinet.

Mitch just laughs. "You kids get all comfy cozy in your big ol' house and you completely forget that Tom owns every single one of you." He points to Tatiana. "Now you're a smart girl. You take care of those people down in the cellar and Tom will take good care of you."

She just nods, and then as quickly as they came, the three men exit, and the moving truck rumbles down the quiet street. For all the neighbors know, we just had a piece of furniture delivered . . . perhaps a bed or a hot tub — not a couple dozen human slaves.

CHAPTER 14

"**W**hat happened to him?" Ruby asks as she and Desiree join us in the kitchen where Jimmy, still wearing a bloody T-shirt, is pressing a dish towel to his bleeding nose.

"Mitch was here," Tatiana says somberly.

"He roughed Jimmy up," Kandy adds.

"And dropped off a bunch of people," I say quietly.

"A bunch of people?" Desiree looks into the great room. "Huh?"

"They're in the basement," Tatiana explains.

"Why'd Mitch bring them here?" Ruby asks.

"Because one of Tom's sweatshops got closed down last week," Jimmy tells her.

"But why *here*?" Ruby persists.

"Because this is Tom's house and because Tom didn't have any other place for them." Jimmy leans over to spit some blood into the sink. "Even though Tom assured me this house was going to be different."

"Yeah, he promised this house was going to be special." Ruby frowns.

"Since when has Tom kept a promise?" Tatiana says bitterly.

"Get over it," Jimmy says. "Besides, you girls need to get

ready. The ride will be here at seven. And you know how it goes if you're late."

Seeing the time, the girls scurry away, and now it's just Jimmy and me in the kitchen. "What about those people? Down in the basement?"

"What about them?" He scowls as he throws the bloody towel into the sink.

"There were children with them. And they all looked pretty hungry."

"So?" He touches the lump rising on his forehead and winces.

I hurry to get some ice out of the freezer and wrap some of it in a paper towel, then hand it to Jimmy. "That might keep the swelling down."

"Thanks."

"Do you care if I take them some food?" I ask cautiously.

He shrugs. "Whatever." He trudges over to the couch where he turns on the TV.

Feeling like I've gotten the green light, I grab a laundry basket and quickly load it with everything I can find, which isn't really much. And when I'm done, I've pretty much cleaned out the food supply. I even put in the jar of salsa Tatiana confiscated from me. I figure these people need it more than I do right now.

I glance over to where Jimmy is slumped on the couch. He is so oblivious to me that I almost wonder if I could make a break for it. Although without the keys in his pocket, it would be almost impossible.

Not wanting to disturb Jimmy from his funk, I try the doorknob to the basement and am surprised to discover the double-keyed dead bolt is unlocked. Do the people down there realize they could get out and come up here? Not that it would do them much good. Although I'd think with their numbers alone, if we really made a plan, we might be able to overpower Jimmy and the others. Except that he has that nasty little stun gun — and who knows what other weapons he might have. Still, it's something to consider. But first these people need food. If we're to stage a rebellion, they should be in better shape.

I carefully make my way down the steep stairs. It's so quiet that I almost wonder if they've escaped somehow. But then I see them. It looks like they've divided into two separate groups. The Hispanics, who seem to outnumber the Asians, are clustered in the couch area where some of the children are hunkered down in front of the TV. The Asian group is gathered over in the bed area, whispering among themselves.

I set the basket of food on the coffee table, and I can see the eager interest in their eyes, but no one makes a move. "This food is for everyone," I say slowly. "To share." But I can tell by their blank expressions that they don't understand. "Does anyone here speak English?"

An Asian girl who appears to be about my age comes over. "I do."

So I explain that this is all the food I can get at the moment. "You'll have to make it last. And everyone will have to share." She translates for me and I learn her name is Lek and that she and the others in her group are from Thailand.

Now I decide to try out my Spanish. I've had three years and apparently it's sufficient because the Hispanic people nod gratefully. I tell them that I will try to help them but I can't promise anything. "You'll just have to be strong," I say to Lek. "And pray to God to send help." Then after I try to say the Spanish version of this, I see more nodding. And some of them say "sí" and "amen."

"Can you get dish?" Lek cups her hands, pantomiming sipping. "To drink?" she says hopefully. "We have water." She points to the bathroom.

"Yes." I nod eagerly, promising to return with some cups.

I go back to the kitchen and hunt around until I find a package of red plastic cups as well as paper plates. I also take a roll of paper towels and a can opener and a few other things that might be useful down there. Then, feeling inspired by their sweet gratitude as I deliver these items, I want to help even more. So I go up and down the stairs numerous times, taking towels and soap and a box of bandages as well as some sheets and blankets I find in another linen closet. I even scavenge some extra pillows from the sofa upstairs. I want to do all I can to make these unfortunate people comfortable while they're here. After the jaded cynicism I've witnessed in this house, their enthusiasm and appreciation is refreshing.

"Are you down there, Serena?" Jimmy yells from the top of the stairs.

"Yes." I hurry back upstairs.

"You want me to lock you down there with the refugees?" he asks in a grumpy tone.

I shake my head. "I was just trying to help them."

"Well, I'm locking up. Now." He snaps the dead bolt closed, removes the key chain, then drops it in his pocket where I hear it jingle.

I vaguely wonder how difficult it would be to get my hands on those keys. Especially if he and Kandy were totally wasted like I imagine they must be about half of the time.

As I go into the kitchen, I notice that it's past seven now. "Didn't your ride come yet?"

He nods. "It came and it went."

"But you didn't go?"

He points to his face, which still looks a bit gruesome. "You think anyone wants to deal with this ugly mug?"

"Oh . . ." I shrug. "So the girls are gone then?"

"Yeah." He goes back to the couch and, reaching for the remote, starts flipping through the channels. "It's okay. I could use a night off."

I sit down and attempt to make small talk with him, hoping to draw him out and find out more about where he's from and what brought him here, but it's obvious he does not want to talk about himself. He's still ticked at Tom for bringing those people in here. Using some off-color language, he puts down the basement dwellers, talking as if they're just animals.

"It's not like they had a choice about coming here," I say. "They don't have any control over any part of their lives." I sigh. "Just like me . . . and you too, really."

"Yeah, well, Tom acts like I have some control." He changes the channel again. "He puts me in charge and keeps saying things are going to get better. And then he goes and turns this house into a refugee center." He swears again. "How am I supposed to take care of everyone?"

I consider reminding him that I'm the one who did all the caretaking tonight but then remember those keys in his pocket and that I'm supposed to be winning his trust.

"Anyway, I might as well forget about it. It's not like I can change anything." He leans back and lets out a weary sigh. "Hey, I haven't seen this film in ages."

Seeing that it's an action flick with way too much violence, I excuse myself, but I'm not sure what to do. Although I'd love to explore the house to see if I can find a weakness to escape from, I do not want to make him suspicious.

I go into the kitchen and pretend to be straightening things up. And as I take a towel out to the laundry room, I try the door to the garage, hoping that in all the activity, someone might've forgotten to lock it. Unfortunately, that is not the case.

It feels strange to be moving around the house at this time of night. But I'm still being careful. I don't want to draw attention. I'm hoping that Jimmy will forget all about me. Or maybe he'll go to sleep. Or better yet, he'll decide to go to his room and get high. I'm thinking if I just lay low, this might be my lucky night.

To kill time, I take a long shower and then just hang out in the bathroom for a while. As I come out, I spot Jimmy still on the couch, still blankly staring at the TV. So I go into my bedroom, where I pace back and forth, trying to make a plan . . . to figure out exactly how I will make my big break tonight. My opportunities, not to mention my days, are limited. Now if only Jimmy would cooperate with my plans.

To distract myself, I start reading one of Ruby's books, but it's hard to focus on the words as I imagine myself sneaking through the house and finding my way of escape. My best plan would be to break free on my own. If I can do that, I will run directly to whichever house looks the safest and I'll knock on the door, and when it's answered, I'll quickly explain my situation and my need for their help and protection. If they're good people, they will take me into their house. And then I will beg them not to contact the local police. I'll try to make them understand that could backfire.

But I will ask them to call Mom. I want her to know exactly where I am and what's going on. After that, I'm sure she'll call the FBI or whoever investigates crimes involving human trafficking. Because I want it to be handled right. I want for everyone who's behind this nasty web of greed and deceit to get what they deserve. I want the ones who are trapped here to have the chance to go free—to get help and find a better life.

I feel so hopeful that I'm actually imagining the conversation I'll have with Mom tonight, when to my complete dismay and disappointment, I hear a noise. I look up to see Jimmy peering into my room, and without saying a word, he slams and locks the door. Just like that, my great escape plans go up in smoke.

Despite my resolve to remain strong, tears of despair slip down my cheeks. Maybe if I'd sneaked around a little more, I could've made it upstairs unobserved. Or maybe I'd have found Jimmy sleeping. Maybe I blew it by not being more persistent. This only makes me cry harder. I'd like to say I'm stronger than this by now, but the truth is, I'm not.

Once again, I know my only recourse is to pray and cry out to God. And my only refuge is to keep trusting in God. So that's what I do. Really, what else can I do? After a while I feel somewhat recovered. Eventually I'm even able to pray, just like I do every night, for everyone in this house.

God, please help and bless each and every person being held here, including the twenty-three women and children now residing in the basement. I'm sure their lives are in much greater peril than my own.

As darkness comes, I sense a familiar nagging voice trying to sneak into my heart again. This is nothing new, and most of the time I can quell this voice by quietly singing praise songs or repeating Bible verses in my head. But tonight I feel so tired . . . so disheartened and discouraged as I recall the hopeless expressions of the people in the basement. Their helplessness only reminds me of how vulnerable we all are.

This persuasive voice is urging me to question God and to doubt his goodness. It whispers into my spirit, warning me to suspect the worst and to prepare myself for the likelihood that I will never escape my captors. It is telling me that God has turned his back on me . . . that I am doomed . . . and that it's all my own fault for wanting to become a model . . . and for keeping information from my mother.

Despite the fact that I confessed these very things to God more than a week ago, and I know that God who is faithful and just has already forgiven me, I feel buried in a deep, dark pile of guilt.

Now I dig down, trying to grasp on to my spiritual roots, trying to remember all that I've been taught since I was a little girl. For my whole life, it seems, Mom and I have attended the same church—a church that acknowledges spiritual warfare and a church where the pastor tells us to test spirits, claim God's power over the evil one, and live victoriously with God's help.

Does that mean I've lived my life perfectly since then? That I've never made a bad decision or blown it? Obviously not. But does that make my faith any less real? Of course not. It simply means that my faith is being tested. I get this.

So now as I dwell in this dark place, I feel that I have to stand firmer than ever. I cannot afford the luxury of doubt in this vile, oppressive world. More than ever, I must cling tightly to God. And when I'm too tired to hold on any longer, I must believe that God will hold fast to me. God will not let me go . . . I believe it.

··· [CHAPTER 15] ················

Morning comes with sunshine and a slender ray of new hope for the day. Since tomorrow is Friday, I'm believing that the time is near. God is going to have to intervene for me. I've tried to be patient. I've tried to be faithful. And now I believe that this horrible ordeal will soon be coming to an end. I have to believe it. However, as the morning and my confinement drag on, I feel my faith wavering.

As much as I want to keep a positive attitude, I feel antsy and aggravated—like I want to start slamming my fist through walls. And I even wonder how hard it would be to break out like that. Is it even humanly possible? Or would I end up bloody and broken and so badly messed up that my value would drop and no one would care whether I lived or died?

As the day wears on, so does my patience. Why does it always take so long for Tatiana to come and unlock this door? I so don't want to use the bucket in the closet. So I bang on the door, calling out for someone to let me out.

To my surprise, it's Ruby who comes to my rescue. She says nothing as she opens my door, but as I come into the hallway, I notice she has a blackened eye. "What happened to you?" I ask as I'm on my way to the bathroom.

"Nothing," she says glumly.

I hurry to use the bathroom. And when I come back out, it's all quiet in the house and Ruby is nowhere to be seen. I'm guessing that everyone is still in bed. This could be my big chance. Once again, I go to the laundry room, hoping that the door to the garage is unlocked, but it's still secure. I go over to the glass sliding door that leads to the backyard. Not only does it have security bars on the outside, the door itself has some kind of device to keep it from opening.

What would happen if there were a fire? How would people get safely out of here? And thinking of this inspires an idea. What if I make a fire? What if the smoke alarms started going off and we all had to evacuate? In the scramble, I could take off running.

So now I'm looking around for something to start a fire with. I'm hurrying, rushing back and forth because I'm worried someone will get up and find me before I can set something blazing. But I can't find a single book of matches or a lighter or even two sticks to rub together.

Finally, just as I'm about to give up, I see the stove in the kitchen. Of course! It's only a glass-topped job, but surely it can produce enough heat to cause a fire. I turn on a front element and grab some paper towels, and then seeing the liquor bottles, I decide to help things out by pouring vodka onto some of the paper towels.

As the red circle on the stove grows hotter, I decide to make this appear to be an accident. So I lay the nearly empty bottle of vodka on its side with some paper towels wadded up around it, like someone was doing a bad job of cleaning it up. Then I trail some of the towels onto the red-hot circle and suddenly it begins to smoke.

Feeling victorious and a bit frightened—what if I burn the place down with everyone in here?—I turn to make a run for it. Just as I'm crossing through the living room area, Jimmy emerges from his room.

"What's going on?" he says with a puzzled frown. "Hey, is that smoke I smell?"

I freeze in my steps. "*Smoke?*" I say stupidly.

"Over there." He dashes toward the kitchen and, knowing he's about to witness my failed pyromania attempt at escape, I take off running back to my room. Even with my door closed, I can hear him cussing and yelling. This is not going to go down well. Why did he have to come out just then?

I sit on the mattress, trying to pretend I'm reading one of Ruby's books, but my brain refuses to focus on the lines of words. My heart is pounding and I know it's only minutes until I get what must be coming to me. As I'm flipping through the pages, I notice some writing in the back of the book. Very neatly in small letters it says: Ruth McKay, Nampa, Idaho.

At first I wonder who this Ruth person is, and then I remember that Ruby let it slip that she used to live in Idaho. Is Ruby's real name Ruth McKay? After all, my real name is Simi and they changed it to Serena. Perhaps they keep the first letter of people's names the same. For some reason this is encouraging.

"Get out here, Serena!" Jimmy opens my door with a flushed face and an enraged expression. "Now!"

I stand up and slowly make my way toward him.

"Move it!" He reaches out and slaps me hard across the face, then shoves me up against the door jam, swearing at me.

Holding my arms over my face, I yell out, reminding him that I'm not supposed to be bruised. Then he slams my back against the wall, and with his face just inches from mine, he screams the worst profanity I've ever heard. I'm splattered with his spittle and his breath smells like rotten garbage.

"Get in there and clean that mess up!" He grabs me by the arm and thrusts me down the hallway. "I'll deal with you later!"

Thanks to Jimmy's firefighting efforts, the mess is even worse than I expected. Water and blackened ashes are all over the place. I find dirty towels in the laundry room to mop it up with. Just as I'm finishing, Jimmy returns with Tatiana in tow. "I blame you as much as I blame Serena for this," he yells at Tatiana. "It's your job to keep an eye on her and she's out—"

"I didn't let her out," Tatiana retorts.

"Then who did?"

Tatiana glares at me. What does she want me to say? Or not say? I have no idea.

"Who let you out?" Jimmy points his finger at me, jabbing it into my chest.

"I'm not sure," I mutter. "I was . . . uh . . . asleep."

He raises his fist like he's going to smack me.

"Leave her alone," Tatiana says in a blasé tone. "You know she's supposed to look good for her date with Mr. T tomorrow."

Now Jimmy turns to Tatiana and slams his fist straight into her face. I'm so shocked I let out a scream. "Get out of here!" He swears at both of us.

I head back to my room, but hearing a scuffle I turn around to see that Tatiana is fighting back. Is this my big chance? I run back, hoping I can help Tatiana against Jimmy. We can pin him down and—

I freeze when Jimmy's stun gun appears. He's got Tatiana by one arm, and before I can say or do anything, he presses the Taser into her neck. She lets out a scream and instantly begins to shake, falling to the floor, where she continues to tremble violently. I run to her side, worried that she's having a seizure, and then her body goes limp.

"Help me pick her up," Jimmy commands. But I feel like I can't move, like I'm in shock. What if she's dead?

I put a hand on her arm, peering at her pale face. "Are you okay?"

"Move it," he growls. When I look up, I see his Taser aimed just inches from me. "Or you wanna be next?"

He grabs her bare feet. "Get that end," he commands. I've barely gotten ahold of her lifeless arms and he's already dragging her down the hallway. I stumble to keep up. "You two are bunking together." He swears as he releases her on the bedroom floor, letting her drop with a heavy clunk. Then he slams the door and the dead bolt snaps shut.

I get the pillow to tuck under her head and, noticing that she's trembling slightly, I remember the treatment for shock. I get the blanket from the bed and lay it over her. At least she's alive.

Now I sit on the floor and close my eyes and pray that she'll be okay. I have no idea what kind of damage a stun gun can do, but between her tremors and her clammy, pale skin, I'm concerned. However, if she needs medical attention, I know she won't get it. All I can do is pray.

After what seems a long while, she slowly regains consciousness, and when she's able to sit, I offer her a drink from my water bottle. She's still a little disoriented, but her senses gradually come back to her. And she begins to quietly call Jimmy all sorts of profane names, saying how much she hates him.

"I'm sorry. I didn't mean for you to get hurt because of me."

She shrugs as she leans back against the wall. "I shouldn't

have let Ruby unlock your door in the first place." She touches the red Taser mark on her neck and winces. Then she feels her lower lip that is badly swollen.

I offer her the water bottle again and she takes a small sip. "What did you do anyway?" She peers curiously at me. "Jimmy said you were trying to burn the whole freaking house down."

So I explain my futile plan. "I wanted the smoke alarms to go off . . . so everyone would have to evacuate."

"And you could run away."

"Yeah."

"And seriously, how far do you think you'd have gotten?" she asks in a hopeless way.

"Home."

"That's optimistic . . . if not delusional."

"I have a plan. I think I could accomplish it. My mom would help me."

She shrugs. "Yeah, well, you're lucky to have someone who cares about you. Not everyone is so fortunate."

I peer at her, wondering once again what brought her here. "Even if you don't have a *real* home to go to, wouldn't you rather be free . . . wouldn't it be better than living like this?"

She glares at me. "*Free?* Are you really that stupid?"

"Freedom is stupid?"

"Do you honestly think there's any place we can go and be free anymore?"

I nod. "Sure. Why not?"

She waves her hands in exasperation. "Because they are everywhere."

I know she means Tom's associates, but I'm still confused. "But you move away . . . go to another state."

"Aren't *you* from another state?" she says.

"Yes, but —"

"But you just don't get it, do you?"

"I'm not sure what you mean."

"I mean this is big business, Serena. Big money-making business. In the Portland metro area alone, there are probably thousands of people connected to guys like Tom. They trade us around like livestock. And if something goes wrong or if someone runs away, the thugs work together. They help each other."

"You make it sound like they rule the world."

"They rule the underworld. And the underworld rules the rest of the world."

"That's probably how it seems to —"

"That's how it is! The sooner you get that, the better off you'll be. And then you won't go around trying to burn down what is probably the best place you'll end up in."

Now she's agitated and on her feet, pacing back and forth and swearing like a sailor again. It's clear I need to change my tactics if I'm going to get anywhere with her. She's so hopeless. Somehow I've got to convince her that there's a way out of this slavery racket. I'm trying to remember what the woman who spoke to our school said about human trafficking last year. Surely she had answers. Suggestions for ways to end the madness.

"What about safe houses?" I ask suddenly.

"Huh?" She pauses in front of the window, staring out the same way I do much of the time. "What are you yammering about?"

"Safe houses," I say. Besides trying to bring human trafficking to our attention, I now remember how that speaker wanted to raise money for safe houses. So surely they must exist . . . somewhere. "Those are places where girls like you or Ruby or Kandy or Desiree can go to get help. Places where you're

protected and given new identities, and I'm sure they have counseling and stuff."

"Right." She turns around with a scowl. "And they probably hand out money and new cars and paid vacations to Honolulu too."

"Okay, I'll admit that I don't know that much about safe houses. But I do know there are good people out there. People who are ready to lend a hand. Even my church would help out if someone really needed it." Now I tell her about how our church has assisted homeless families and women in abusive relationships. "I'm certain they'd help with girls caught in trafficking too."

"What about girls who don't want help?" she says bitterly.

"Like you?"

With her arms folded in front of her, she glares at me.

"Or do you mean girls like Kandy?" I persist, hoping not to press her hot buttons.

She rolls her eyes toward the ceiling. "Yeah, well, Kandy likes her life just the way it is. She gets high in exchange for . . . all of this. Someday she'll wake up dead."

"Will she die from an overdose? Or will she be murdered?"

Tatiana shrugs.

"How do you guys endure this?"

Tatiana looks like she wants to hit me, and I know I should be a little more cautious. Except that I feel desperate to get through to her.

"I know you're tough. Probably the toughest girl in this house. And you're good at pretending this life is no big deal. But I also know you're definitely not happy in this life."

She leans against the wall, sliding back down to the floor and pulling her knees up in front of her, almost in a fetal position. I don't want to push this girl too hard, but I don't want to lose this moment either.

"And I know Ruby isn't happy. Neither is Desiree. How can any of you be? You have no rights. You get beat up. They'll use you and lose you . . . and go out and find another girl."

She lifts her head, giving me a bored look, as if nothing I'm saying even registers with her. "Sure, you can come in here and act like you have all the answers, Serena. And you can pretend you're better than us . . . and like you're going to escape this hellhole." She narrows her eyes. "But in the end, you're stuck here. Just like us."

"But I won't be—"

"*Listen!*" She points her finger at me. "Once you've spent some time with Mr. T *tomorrow night*"—she shakes her head in a dismal way—"well, maybe by then you'll understand how we feel—what our lives are really like. Until then, you should just keep your big mouth shut!"

There's a long silent pause now. Her words have a chilling effect on me and I'm sure she knows it. She knows how much I'm dreading tomorrow. Yet somehow I want to convey confidence. And I want her to trust me . . . so she will help me.

"I know you think it's hopeless," I say quietly. "But I still believe God is going to spare me." I brace myself for her sarcastic laughter, which comes as predicted, and then I continue. "I know, you think I'm crazy, but I've really been praying. And I honestly believe God is going to get me out of here—*before* Mr. T. Somehow I'm going to get out of here."

"Like your little torch-the-house escape plan?" She looks disgusted. "That worked so well for you."

"At least I haven't given up. Not like some people."

Her dark eyes narrow. "Are you saying I've given up?"

"Haven't you?"

She gently runs her finger back and forth over her swollen lip. It looks like she's thinking . . . I can only hope. Without saying anything, I just wait, silently praying that God will help me to get through to her.

"You seem like an intelligent person to me," I finally break the silence. Okay, this is a tactic I've learned from watching Dr. Phil. When he wants to get someone's attention, someone who's being difficult or hard, he will catch them off guard with a compliment. It's worth a try.

Her eyes flicker with interest.

"And despite everything you've been through, and I'm sure it's a lot, you still seem like a strong person. Like you really don't want to be anyone's slave. Like you could still be in charge of your life . . . well, as much as possible . . . under the circumstances."

"What's your point?" She gives me her bored look again, but at least I know it's an act now.

"My point is that you could have a really great life, if you wanted it." Now I stand and start pacing, gathering my words. "Seriously, Tatiana, you're smart. I can tell. I know you could finish school or get your GED. Then you could go to college and you could probably get a really good job." I pause to watch her expression and I can tell she's listening. "And maybe you'd meet a great guy . . . or even get married and have—"

"A great guy who wants to marry someone like me?" She narrows her eyes. "Get real."

"It could happen—everything I just said could become a reality. If you believe in yourself."

"What I *can't* believe is how someone like you—someone who claims to know all about God—can act like a girl like me can turn it around so easily. Seriously, are you that naive? Do you honestly think I'll ever have anything besides this kind of life? I deserve what I have, Serena. Don't you get that?"

"But God has so much more for—"

"No! According to what I've heard about your Mr. Goody Two-Shoes God, he is not real fond of bad girls like me. He has fire and brimstone for sinners and—"

"That is where you are dead wrong," I cut her off. "God is *not* like that at all. He loves us all so much that he sent his son, Jesus Christ, to earth. And Jesus, who has the same power as God, gave up everything in order to forgive us and restore us to God. And just so you know, while Jesus was living on earth, he reached out to *everyone*. I mean, he was friends with people from all walks. He hung with hookers and thieves and all sorts of losers."

She looks surprised by my unexpected sermon. I'm actually a little surprised myself, but I think maybe God helped me with those words.

I go over to the window and look out. I want to give her time to chew on what I just said. And as I stand there, I pray for God to do a miracle in Tatiana's heart. Or at least to make her trust me.

fter what feels like nearly an hour, Tatiana speaks up. "Do you honestly believe what you just said? About God and Jesus?"

"Absolutely," I assure her. "Every word of it."

"But how do you know it's really true?"

"You mean that God loves you and wants to forgive you?"

"Yeah."

"All my life, my mom and I have gone to a church where they preach the Bible. So I grew up hearing all of that. And I'll admit I went through a rough spell a few years ago, when I doubted everything, including God. But then I was at a summer camp where I experienced God's love and forgiveness for myself, and it all just connected and made sense. And I completely committed my life to him. Ever since then I've been reading the Bible and experiencing these things for myself."

"And what you said about Jesus being with hookers and all that? Is that really in the Bible? Is it true?"

"Absolutely. Jesus was really drawn to people with problems. He reached out to anyone who was down and out. I swear it's true. And that's how God is too. He's just waiting for us to realize how much we need him. Sometimes you have to get really low to reach the place where you can look up. God wants us to be so needy that we cry out to him for help and—"

"And you've been doing that, *right*?" Skepticism creeps back into her voice.

"Yeah . . ." I brace myself for her attack.

Tatiana's dark eyes glimmer with meanness as she waves her hand toward me. "But you're still here, Serena. And your date with Mr. T is still tomorrow."

"It's not over yet," I say calmly. "I'm trusting God's goodness to take care of me."

To my surprise, her expression softens slightly. "I'm sorry. I shouldn't pick on you just because you have faith. And I shouldn't keep throwing Mr. T in your face. You'll get that soon enough."

I'm touched that she actually seems sorry. But at the same time, her jabs about my upcoming date are unnerving. "Hey, I can't deny that I'm in a low place right now. Seriously, since being kidnapped and brought here, I've never cried and prayed so much in my life. But at the same time, I refuse to quit believing that God's going to help me."

"Yeah . . . well, that's cool . . . for you I mean. Whatever it takes to get you through the day."

"Prayer does get me through the day. But as much as I've been praying for myself to get out of here, I've also been praying for everyone else in this house. Including you." I sigh. "I even pray for Jimmy, although it'll be harder now that he's turned into such a bully."

Tatiana doesn't respond.

"And just so you know, when I *do* make it out of here, I plan to go to the FBI or some form of trusty law enforcement. And I will tell them everything I know about everyone and everything that's going on here. Including the twenty-three women and children being held down in the basement right now."

"You mean *if* you escape. But just so you know, *if* you do get out of here somehow, which I doubt, this place will be cleared out within the hour," Tatiana says glumly.

"How is that even possible?"

"Tom's connections. Believe me, Serena, I know what I'm talking about. That's just one more motivation for us to keep you safely here. We don't want to leave. We like this house. It's a lot better than the other places."

"But what about the people downstairs? They probably don't like it. And what about Jimmy being so upset that Tom sent them here? Doesn't that change things?"

Tatiana frowns. "Maybe . . . maybe not . . . it's hard to say what's around the next corner. And people come and go. No matter where you are, nothing stays the same for long."

"How can you stand to live like this?" I say urgently. "Never knowing if you're going to be thrown into the back of a truck and sent off somewhere else? And what if you got shipped off to a foreign country? It's like you have absolutely no control over anything."

She makes a slight shrug.

"Are you saying you're okay with all that?"

"Of course not. But what choice do I have?"

"You could help me get out of here!"

She laughs, and although it sounds hollow, there's no meanness in it this time. "Look around you, Serena. How are you going to break out?"

"I don't know. But somehow I will." Now I lock gazes with her. "And when I do get out of here, do you even want me to send back help for you?"

She sadly shakes her head. "Don't waste your time. I'm sure we'll all be long gone by the time your so-called help arrives."

I bite my lip and try to figure out an answer to this. I know what she's saying and I hate to admit that it makes sense . . . but it does. "Well, as hopeless as everything seems, I'm still praying," I say finally. "God is bigger and stronger than all of this. I believe he wants to help the helpless."

I pick up a book that Ruby loaned me, sitting in a stack with the other two. "I know Ruby's real name. And where she used to live, too. I plan to let the authorities know. So they can help her."

Tatiana looks doubtful. "How would you know her name or where she's from?"

I point to the book. "It's in there. She's Ruth McKay from Nampa, Idaho."

Tatiana shrugs. "Doesn't matter."

"Maybe, but it might be useful in finding Ruby's mom. And I'm sure she must care about her daughter. My information will give her a better idea of how to search for Ruby. Anyway, it can't hurt."

"Ruby does need to get out of here," Tatiana says unexpectedly.

I nod eagerly. "Yeah. We all do."

"But especially Ruby." Tatiana looks concerned. "I know this is going to kill her. She's not strong enough."

I feel a lump in my throat now. Who is strong enough?

"And thanks for not telling Jimmy that Ruby's the one who let you out this morning. She woke me up . . . said she heard you yelling and I just ignored her. I'm sure that's why she came down here and let you out. But Jimmy would've beaten her if he'd known. She already had a pretty rough night last night."

"I noticed." It's incredibly reassuring to see how much Tatiana cares about Ruby. "Can't you see why I want to help her?"

She nods.

"Why I want to help all of you." I pause. "Maybe if you told me your real name, I could help you, too."

Tatiana just shrugs. "It's not like it's going to make any difference one way or the other. I don't care if you know my real name."

"Great."

"Tamara Bishop. I'm from the Seattle area."

"So how'd you get to this place?" I try to make this sound like a casual question. Like two friends just having a conversation.

"Same old story as a lot of girls my age."

"How old are you anyway?"

"Seventeen."

"So by same old story, you mean that you ran away from home and Jimmy found you and took you in?"

"No. Not *that* same story. Not exactly anyway. It started happening last year. Although, come to think of it, my parents and I hadn't gotten along for years. My older brother and sister were out of the house. And suddenly it was like my parents were so obsessed with their own lives that they kinda forgot about me. And I'll admit that I probably did the wrong things to get their attention. When I got in trouble, they would get really mad and ground me for like forever. And they'd take away my phone. And sure, I might've deserved it a couple of times, but most of the time it seemed unfair. Like it was just more convenient for them to lock me up than to have a real conversation." She kind of laughs. "Ironic, huh? I leave my parents to get some freedom and wind up here."

I just nod.

"Last winter, right after I turned seventeen, I felt pretty grown up, like I didn't need my parents anymore. In December, I stayed out too late and got grounded and lost my phone again. But I was still allowed online. It was winter break and I was surfing the net and messing with my Facebook, posting some pretty cool pics, and waiting for someone to respond."

"Yeah . . . I know how that goes." Man, do I.

"So, right before Christmas, I met this really gorgeous guy on Facebook. Jesse was so cool. And it seemed like we really connected. He said all the right things, flattered my ego, told me I was pretty and smart and interesting. And I stupidly ate it up. As our relationship progressed, he sent me photos of himself—and man, was he hot. I sent him similar photos of me." She rolls her eyes upward. "Photos that never should've seen the light of day. Jesse told me I was hot and that he wanted to be with me. I honestly thought we were in love."

"What happened?"

"We kept chatting and sending photos for a few weeks. Jesse told me that he was twenty and in his second year in a private college near Portland. But he said he was tired of school and planned to take a break during winter term. He said he wanted to be in the sunshine. And that he wanted us to be together. He told me his family was rich and he could take care of me. He sent me these fabulous photos of his parents' vacation home on the big island in Hawaii, and he invited me to go with him to stay there. He said we could hide out until I turned eighteen."

"And?"

"I knew it was wrong. But I was still mad at my parents. And everything sounded so perfect. So I told him yes, and he sent me an e-ticket to Portland. He said we'd meet up there, and then we'd fly on to Hawaii together. It was going to be so amazing." She sighs almost as if she still believes it could be true.

"What happened?"

"I spent a few days acting like the perfect girl, you know, to get my parents to trust me more. Mom even let me have my phone back. I pretended to be going to school just like any other day, but instead I went to the airport and boarded the flight to Portland. When my flight arrived, Jesse texted me to meet him down in baggage claim. He said our flight wasn't leaving for a few hours and he wanted to take me to lunch in Portland." Her mouth twists to one side. "I was so naive and gullible back then."

Somehow, maybe it's the snake tattoo or her severe black hair, but it's hard to believe Tatiana was ever that naive. Just the same, I nod.

She's standing again, walking as she tells her story and, judging by her expression, it's like she's back there, experiencing it all over again. "So I'm all happy and excited to meet my dream guy. I stop by the bathroom to make sure my hair and makeup are perfect." She touches her hair. "My hair was long and brown then. A lot like yours. So, feeling good, I go down to baggage claim and outside to where Jesse planned to pick me up on the street. And I spot the car he'd described perfectly to me. I see what I'm sure is him, waving over the top of the car, and I hear him call out my name as the car slowly approaches."

She pauses, touching her swollen lower lip, but her eyes are far away. "I can't see inside the car's tinted windows, but I'm not concerned. I figure this is a good way to keep from being spotted, and by now I'm getting worried my parents might've figured out that I'm missing. So I hurry over to the car and the next thing I know, the back door opens and as I lean in, I'm snatched right off the street and pulled into the car. So fast that I don't even have time to scream."

She shakes her head. "Although, to be honest, I don't think I would've screamed anyway. At that point I just thought it was some kind of stupid joke Jesse was pulling. But I barely had time to look around the car before I was blindfolded and handcuffed and gagged. But I never saw Jesse in that car. Just a couple of middle-aged men. Jesse wasn't there." Her eyes look close to tears as she turns away, going over to the window again, her hands clutching the sill.

"Do you think Jesse was even real?" I ask quietly.

She laughs, but it's full of hardness.

"No." I answer my own question. "Of course he wasn't real."

The room grows quiet and I'm imagining Tatiana, or Tamara, being blindsided and abducted in a way that sounds very similar to how I was kidnapped in LA, and I feel even more empathy toward her. "And that was how long ago?"

"Six . . . seven months. I quit counting after a while."

"Did you ever try to get away?"

"Oh, sure. When I wasn't drugged." And now she pulls up her T-shirt and shows me some scars, explaining how she got each one of them. "Besides that, they threatened to post all my *overexposed* photos on the Internet and send them to my parents." She shrugs. "For some reason that was even more disturbing than being beaten."

"Really? I don't think photos on the Internet would stop me from trying to escape."

"That's because you don't know how these guys work." She narrows her eyes as she looks down at the rug. "Don't kid yourself, Serena. There's nothing you can do to stop this machine. Once you're in, you're in for good."

"Not if God rescues me."

Tatiana looks tired. "You know, for your sake, I wish that was true." She nods to the mattress. "Mind if I take a little nap? That stun gun kinda took the stuffing out of me."

She flops down on the mattress and closes her eyes. Her nose is about twice as big as normal and the red blotch on her neck looks painful, but she seems oblivious to these wounds as she slips off to sleep.

As much as I appreciate that she trusts me enough to tell me her sad story, it doesn't make me feel one bit better about this situation. Hearing her perspective makes everything look even more hopeless and frightening than before. Not only that, but I'm painfully aware that I don't have much time left. If I don't escape this place, I will come face-to-face with Mr. T tomorrow night. *God help me!*

CHAPTER 17

Later in the afternoon, Ruby comes to our room. "I can't let you guys out," she says quietly as she shoves a fast-food bag and a couple of water bottles toward me. "Jimmy's watching me like a hawk." She cringes to see Tatiana's swollen lip. "You okay?"

"Just great," Tatiana answers with her usual sarcasm.

"Thanks for not ratting me out," Ruby tells me as she backs away.

"No problem." I thank her for the provisions.

"And I'll tell Jimmy your face is too messed up to go out with us tonight," Ruby assures Tatiana.

"Thanks for small favors," Tatiana mumbles.

As we eat our cold burgers and fries, I ask Tatiana if she thinks there's any way to break out of here. "Like maybe we could kick through the walls."

She points to our bare feet. "Seriously? You think we could kick through walls?"

I shrug. "How about breaking a window and calling for help? Wouldn't the neighbors do something?"

"You really don't get it, do you?"

I study her closely, trying to determine if she truly believes it's impossible to break out or if she has simply given up. "It's just a house. Not a prison."

"Then why are you still here?"

I go over to the window, and as I munch on a fry, I study the double panes and then look out into the backyard like I've done so many times before. Usually I'm daydreaming about going home, seeing Mom and Michelle and going to youth group and even babysitting the twins. It all sounds so good now. If only I could get out of here.

"I really think I could break the glass out with my fist," I say absently. "Or maybe with my head. Maybe if I got a running start, bounced from the mattress and—"

Tatiana drowns me out with her laughter, and this time it almost sounds genuine. "Now that'd be using your head."

I turn to look at her. "I don't want to go tomorrow."

"I know you don't," she answers solemnly.

"So I'm warning you," I say as I sit back down. "If I see a chance to run for it, I'm taking it."

"Good luck."

I stare at her. "Really, do you mean that? Or is it just more of your sarcasm?"

She shrugs. "I guess I mean it. You deserve to get out of here."

"And you don't?"

"I don't know what I deserve."

"You don't deserve to be a slave. No one does. And no one should be held against her will. Slavery was abolished a long time ago."

"So they say." She eats the last of her burger and crumbles the paper into a wad that she shoots into the bag. Then to distract ourselves we start playing a makeshift game of basketball, taking turns shooting wadded-up paper balls from different parts of the room into the bag. But eventually we tire of the silly game, and then I offer to read to her from one of the books Ruby loaned me. To my surprise, she seems eager to listen and I make it through quite a few chapters before I realize she's fallen asleep . . . with a small smile on her lips. Go figure.

. . . .

The next morning, our door is unlocked and it feels much earlier than usual.

"Everybody up and at 'em," Jimmy says cheerfully, smiling as if he hadn't just been a mean brute yesterday. But then he wrinkles his nose. "Man, it reeks in here." He moves back into the hallway.

"What'd you expect?" Tatiana growls at him as she stands. "I wish someone would lock you in here for a couple of days."

"Ooh, sounds like someone got up on the wrong side of the bed this morning."

I sense Tatiana tensing up and wonder if she's about to attack him. I'd be happy to back her, except I'm worried he'll pull out his stun gun again. So I toss her a look. "Go ahead and use the bathroom first if you want. I don't mind waiting."

She rolls her eyes but doesn't argue.

"And you can go use the upstairs bathroom," he tells me. "Take a good long shower. I'll send Desiree in there with some things you'll need to make yourself more presentable." He gives me a disgusted look. "This is going to be an all-day project."

Ignoring his insult, I head upstairs and go into the bathroom. This one is bigger and nicer than the one downstairs. Once again, I help myself to the bath products. As I scrub off what feels like a lot of grime, I can tell that I've lost weight—weight I didn't really need to lose. But considering the small rations of food I've been given, it's not surprising. Still, it reminds me of the captives downstairs. How long could they possibly last on what I gave them two days ago? Trying not to fret over them, I say a quick prayer as I shampoo my hair. And because it's been pretty tangled, I apply a generous amount of conditioner and take time to work it in thoroughly. Not for my date tonight, but because I plan to be free before the day ends.

"Here's a razor," Desiree yells as she sticks her hand into the shower with a purple razor. "Put it to good use and then give it back to me when you're done. Don't think you can hold on to it to use as a weapon later. *Understand?*"

"Yeah . . . thanks."

"Mr. T likes his girls clean and sleek and pretty," she says.

"Hopefully he likes them skinny, too."

She pulls open the curtain and peers at me, then shrugs. "You'll be fine."

"Maybe," I say as I shave my leg. "But the shortage of food sure saps my energy. You think Mr. T is going to like that?"

I can see through the translucent shower curtain that she's sitting on the toilet seat. "I'll tell Jimmy to call out for pizza," she says absently.

Desiree remains at her post until I'm done. As I reach for a towel, I obediently hand the razor back to her. "Thanks."

"Dry off and then come to my room." She studies me. "I'm supposed to work magic on you today." She reaches over to finger my hair. "Jimmy said not to mess with your hair . . . yet."

"Yet?"

"Well, if we decide to keep you—I mean, after your date—we'll have to change your hair. Jimmy says blonde, but

I'm thinking you'd be good as a redhead." She pats her own blonde hair and I suspect she wouldn't want to have two blondes in the house.

"Why can't I just keep my hair like this?"

She laughs. "I'll let you figure out the answer to that one yourself, *Serena*."

As she leaves, I get it. In the same way they change your name, they change your hair. It's to make girls less recognizable . . . just in case someone is looking for them. As I towel-dry my hair, I wonder if anyone is actually looking for any of these girls. Does anyone even care? Or do they assume they are dead?

However, I feel certain my mom is looking for me. I know it. I just wish I hadn't kept my plans for meeting with Marcia and Bryce a secret. If only I'd told her what I was doing, maybe I wouldn't have wound up here at all.

I find a terry-cloth robe in the bathroom, and since my little black dress, which looks more like a little black rag, is filthy, I borrow it. But instead of going directly to Desiree's room, I wander down the hallway, peering at everything, wondering if there is some way to escape that's been overlooked.

"What're you doing out here?" Kandy snaps at me as she emerges from her room with a suspicious look.

"Looking for Desiree," I say innocently.

"Her room is right down there." Kandy glares at me. "And you know it."

"I forgot," I say as I head back to Desiree's room.

Kandy stops me, putting a firm hand on my shoulder. "Jimmy said to keep a close eye on you today. He said not to trust you any further than we can throw you. So I'm warnin' you, *girlfriend*, any monkey business and I'll be the first one to turn you in." She puts her face in my face. *"You get me?"*

I nod. "Sure."

Now she puts on her saccharine smile and gives me a friendly pat on the back. "Well, just as long as you understand, we'll all be fine and dandy."

"Hey," Desiree calls from her room. "You coming or not, Serena?"

"I'm coming." I hurry past Kandy and go into Desiree's room.

"Kandy playing policeman with you?" Desiree asks as she closes the door.

I shrug. "Yeah, I guess."

"She's Jimmy's puppet, you know." Desiree sits down in front of her TV and starts playing a video game.

"Yeah, I kinda figured that out." I sit on the other side of her bed. "They seem to have a connection."

Desiree laughs. "Yeah, the coke connection."

I just watch as she plays the game. I know she's supposed to be giving me some special beauty treatment, but she doesn't seem to be in any more of a hurry than I am. So I study her room, wondering if there's not some way to break out through here. Since we're on the second floor, I'm wondering about the attic. Is there some way to get up there? And if so, would there be a way to get out? Maybe onto the roof and climb down?

"If Tom decides to keep you, they'll try to get you hooked too," she says in a slightly absent way, still focusing on her game.

"Oh?"

"Yeah. They try to get everyone hooked on something. It makes it easier for them. Kinda like babysitters, I guess." She leans to one side as she presses the remote over and over. "Jimmy usually tries to get you on meth . . . you know, 'cause it's cheaper.

But man, I hated that stuff. Weed is better." She pauses again, shooting the monster like she means it. "Just sayin'."

Hearing someone at the door, she tosses the remote and pops over to where I'm sitting. She grabs a brush and pretends to be fussing with my hair as the door opens.

"How's it going?" Jimmy asks with narrowed eyes.

"Fine," Desiree answers.

Jimmy comes over and picks up one of my hands. He studies it and shakes his head. "Mr. T likes French manicures, but I don't know if these nails can be saved."

"Don't worry," Desiree assures him. "I'm on it."

"And she's so pale," he says. "You gonna put some bronzer on her?"

"I said *I'm on it*, Jimmy." She gives him an exasperated look. "You think you can do better, just go ahead and have at it." She holds out the hairbrush to him.

"No, that's okay. I just want to be sure you're really on it. A lot is riding on this deal. I want to make sure that Tom appreciates our work."

"Tom." She rolls her eyes. "Has he gotten rid of all those people in the basement yet?"

Jimmy swears.

"Yeah, I figured."

"I told him to bring some food by," Jimmy says a bit helplessly.

"Speaking of food, Serena is hungry. Sounds like she hasn't eaten in days. Besides the fact you can see her ribs. How's she going to have any energy?"

Jimmy looks concerned now.

"Why don't you send out for pizza?"

He nods, looking slightly nervous. "Yeah. I'll do that."

"Good. And if you don't trust me to fix her up, why don't you get someone else to do it. Like Kandy."

He holds up his hands. "I trust you, Desiree."

"Then get out of here!"

He just laughs as he leaves, but I can tell he's not as secure as he pretends to be. "It must be hard being in charge of this house," I say to Desiree as she returns to her game.

"He gets his payoffs."

"Yeah." I stand and walk around her room, trying to figure out who this girl really is. And while some things I see are disgusting and disturbing, other things seem perfectly normal. "So I realize I might not see you again." I pick up a stuffed blue bear with a pink heart pasted to its chest. It looks like a carnival prize. "And I just want you to know that I appreciate your friendship. I wish I could've gotten to know you better."

She pauses from playing, glancing my way with curiosity, then she returns to her game.

"I was thinking about your situation," I continue. "How your parents had problems . . . and your grandma died . . . and the bad foster care homes . . . and it's all so sad."

"Tell me about it."

"But as sad as it sounds, it doesn't seem nearly as sad as this place."

She stops playing, sets down the remote, and glares at me. "You think this place is bad?"

I shrug. "Yeah. It's bad compared to being free."

"Well, it's nothing compared to *some* places. And after your date with Mr. T . . . well, depending on how that goes, you might be seeing some of those really nasty places. Real soon." She stands and comes over to look at me. "So don't act like we've got it so bad here."

I lock gazes with her. "But wouldn't you rather be free?"

She turns away, going over to her bureau where she's gathering up some things. "We better get to work on you. Jimmy's right. You look pretty bad."

"Thanks." I feign a little laugh. "But considering my living conditions of late, I'm not going to take that too personally."

She instructs me to sit in a chair and proceeds to start working on me. She makes me soak my feet in a tub, then uses exfoliation creams and lotions on the rest of me. But as she does her work, I continue to talk. I tell her the whole story of how I fell for Marcia and Bryce's lies and got kidnapped. "I know it was partly my own fault for being so gullible. But I still hope they get busted."

"Yeah, well, that's probably not going to happen." She's sitting on the floor now, working intently on my feet. "The bad guys always get their way and then they get away."

"Really? Do you honestly believe that?" I'm balancing a bowl of warm sudsy water in my lap, keeping my hands in it to soften them up for my manicure.

"That's how it looks from my end." Desiree's painting my toenails a pale shade of pink. "Problem is, you can never tell they're bad guys. Not in the beginning. They put on their game faces . . . win you over with their smooth-talking charm."

"Is that what happened to you?"

"Yeah." Focused on my toes, she opens up. "I was at the mall with a couple of girlfriends when this guy started hitting on me. I was pretty flattered that he picked me over them. And even though I could tell he was older, I was cool with it. But my friends didn't like him. They said I was stupid to go out with him, but I thought they were just jealous."

She switches to the other foot. "Garrett and I went out a few times. And he was so good to me. For the first time in my life, I felt like someone really cared about me. He took me out and he bought me cool clothes and expensive shoes. Even some diamond earrings. At least he said they were diamonds. I didn't know for sure. But he treated me like a real lady. I felt just like Cinderella."

"Wow, that does sound pretty cool."

"Uh-huh." She returns to the other foot now, applying another coat. "But then one night, Garrett showed up and he was all bummed. He told me he lost his job and that he was broke. I felt so bad for him. Especially after he'd spent so much money on me. I mean, one pair of shoes he bought had cost more than three hundred dollars. I asked him if he could return any of my gifts, but he didn't think the stores would take them back." She shakes her head. "And then he got this idea."

"What kind of idea?"

"He told me he'd been looking in the classified ads for a job and he'd seen an ad for dancers. He told me he was so desperate that he'd actually gone in, but they told him they only wanted girls. Pretty girls. Then he told me how much they got paid, and I couldn't believe it. When he asked me if I was willing to do it — for him — well, how could I say no?"

I nod. "Yeah, I guess that would make sense."

"So pretty soon I was sneaking out of the foster home and dancing at a club to earn money. Garrett talked me into leaving the foster home. And before long, Garrett convinced me I could make even more money . . . you know . . ." She sighs as she switches to the other foot. "And then Garrett told me he was going into the military to earn some money for us. He said it was the Air Force, but I found out later that he was lying. He told me I could stay with friends until he got out and then we'd get back together again. But he really sold me to Tom."

"Garrett sold you to Tom?"

"That's what I heard. Apparently Garrett does it all the time."

"Sells girls?" I try not to show how shocking this sounds.

"Yeah. He meets teen girls at malls. I guess he's got some kind of special radar for picking out the girls who will fall for his tricks. And then he does the same thing—buys them stuff, then tells them he's broke, talks them into working to earn back the money he spent on them . . ." Desiree sighs as she stands and puts the lid back on the polish.

"And then he sells them to Tom?" I say in disgusted disbelief. Somehow, compared to all the stories I've heard, this one seems the worst.

"Yep. That's how he makes his living. Finding girls. Grooming girls. Selling girls." She shakes her head. "Pretty messed up, huh?"

"Yeah."

Now she sits beside me and starts working on my fingernails. As she works, we continue to talk and I discover her real name is Deirdre Emerson and that she was originally from Gresham, which she tells me is near Portland. "Most of the West Coast girls come from the I-5 corridor," she says nonchalantly. "I guess it's just more convenient that way."

It's nearly two and Desiree has just finished up my fingernails when Ruby comes in to announce that there's pizza downstairs.

"Bring some up here," Desiree tells her. "We need to keep working on Serena."

"What about the people in the basement?" I ask Ruby. "Did Jimmy get any food for them?"

Ruby frowns. "Jimmy said he hopes they'll all starve to death."

"Well, that's just wrong," Desiree says.

"Do you think we can sneak anything down to them?" I ask.

"Not with Jimmy parked down there in front of the TV," Ruby tells me.

"What if we had a way to break out of here?" I say quietly.

Now the room, which had seemed so friendly, suddenly turns silent . . . chilly.

"I know you think this isn't as bad as some places," I continue, "but what if there was a place where you would be safe? A place where you would have freedom? Where you could finish school? Go to college? Have a real life? Wouldn't you want that?"

"Yeah . . . I always wanted to go to Disneyland too," Ruby says sadly.

Desiree laughs and runs her fingers through Ruby's hair. "See why I love this little girl? Such a sense of humor."

I point to Ruby's black eye. "But that's not funny."

"Don't you think we'd have gotten out of here if it was possible?" Desiree snarls at me. "Do you honestly think we stay here because we like it?"

I shake my head. "No. But at the same time I believe there's a way out."

"Well, you keep us in the loop," Desiree says. "In the meantime, where's that pizza, Ruby?"

Ruby is still staring at me. Almost like she wants to believe I have some secret plan to free us from this place, like I have some magic key or some free passes to Disneyland. Then she turns and hurries out.

"Don't go getting her hopes up," Desiree hisses at me as soon as Ruby is gone.

"Sorry. But I honestly believe there are alternatives. And I plan to break out of here. Soon."

Desiree laughs again. "Well, the clock is ticking, Serena. Your date with Mr. T is less than five hours away. You think you're going to make your big break before then?"

"If we all worked together, we could take Jimmy. And I'm sure that Tatiana would help too."

"Yeah, right. You mean the same Tatiana who got knocked out by his stun gun yesterday?" Desiree is putting away the manicure stuff. "I heard how that went down."

"But there would be four of us against one."

"Four?" She peers at me. "Tatiana is in lockdown all day. Or didn't you know that?"

"But even if it was just three of us. You and me and Ruby. Against Jimmy and one stun gun, we should be able to —"

"Jimmy isn't limited to one stun gun." She pours the manicure water into the bigger tub. "He has all kinds of stuff."

"But we could catch him off guard."

She holds out the tub of dirty water. "Go dump this and forget about it."

As I take the water from her, I feel certain my plan could work. "Really, Desiree. The three of us could take Jimmy. I know it. He's not that big. If we joined forces, we could —"

"You could do *what*?" Kandy demands as she opens the door.

Desiree doesn't even look surprised. "Hey, Kandy."

Kandy ignores her, pointing at me. *"Do what?"*

"Nothing," I say quickly. "I need to dump this. Excuse me."

But Kandy doesn't budge from blocking the door. "I heard every single word y'all said just now. And I'm telling Jimmy the whole thing."

"Desiree didn't say anything," I counter. "So don't go telling stories on her. I was the one doing all the talking. You can tell Jimmy that."

"Don't worry, I will. And you are toast, girlfriend."

I act nonchalant. "I'm sure Mr. T will appreciate being served toast tonight. Tom ought to like it too."

Kandy just swears at me and then rushes off—I'm sure to tell Jimmy. I go to the bathroom and dump the water in the tub, wondering how much of a problem I've just created. Not so much for myself, but for Desiree and maybe Ruby, too. And hearing Tatiana's in lockdown doesn't help either.

As I stand at the top of the stairs, listening to Kandy ranting to Jimmy about me and Desiree, I wonder if everyone in this house wouldn't be better off if I'd never shown up here. Not that I had a choice in the matter. But it seems that every time I try to help out or plan an escape, it gets all messed up and someone else gets hurt. Once again, I know that all I can do is pray . . . and watch for an opportunity.

CHAPTER 18

Ruby returns with pizza and wide eyes. "Jimmy is really mad," she quietly confides to Desiree. "But he's not going to do anything until you're done with Serena."

"Great." Desiree rolls her eyes as she reaches for a piece of pizza. "Guess I'll just take my time then."

As we eat pizza, I quietly apologize. "I didn't want to get anyone in trouble," I say as Ruby stands guard by the door, watching for Kandy.

"Can't you see it's useless?" Desiree tells me.

"I can see why you need to be careful. It's just that I really want to make my break *before* tonight." I glance at Ruby, thankful she's keeping watch. "Do you think there's any chance I can escape from the car that takes me?"

"What do *you* think?" Desiree twists a piece of cheese around her finger, giving me a "duh" expression.

Remembering how I was transported here and knowing my value as Mr. T's date, I know what she's saying. "Well, I'm going to think of something. I'm going to escape and I'm going to send someone here to help you guys, too."

Desiree just laughs and Ruby nervously peers down the hallway toward the stairs. Then she turns back to me. "I read a story once about a girl who drugged her captor's drink and got away after he passed out."

"Do you think we could drug Jimmy's drink?" I ask hopefully.

"He uses so many drugs it'd probably take a whole pharmacy to knock him out," Desiree says.

"I meant Mr. T," Ruby says quietly to me. "Maybe you can slip something into his drink."

"Even if Serena *could* do that, which is pretty ridiculous, where would she get anything to drug him with in the first place?"

"From Jimmy," Ruby suggests.

"Yeah, right, like that's going to happen. You know Jimmy, always leaving his door unlocked."

Ruby shrugs. "What about Kandy?"

"Kandy would kill anyone who touched her stuff. You know that."

Ruby hurries back into the room and reaches for another piece of pizza, giving us a warning look. It's not long before Kandy appears at the door with a smug look. "Having a little party in here, are we? I wasn't invited."

"Feel free to join us," Desiree tells her. "Maybe you'd like to help Serena with her bronzer."

Kandy rolls her eyes. "Thanks but no thanks."

"Thanks for the pizza, Ruby," Desiree says, almost like a hint for the younger girl to leave and distance herself from us. Ruby seems to get the hint, making a quiet exit, and now Desiree returns to working on me. Neither of us speaks much as she shows me how to apply bronzer and how to keep it from looking weird or streaky. After that's done and has a chance to dry, she sits me down and begins to put some makeup on me.

"I'm not using too much," she explains. "Because Mr. T likes his dates to look sweet and natural."

I grimace but keep my thoughts to myself. Now it's close to five o'clock, and I can tell that Desiree has dragged this out as long as possible, but I'm still in the bathrobe. "So what am I wearing tonight?" I'm imagining some horrible outfit. Probably something strapless and tight.

"Oh, yeah . . . that." She goes to her closet and hands me a plaid pleated skirt, a navy vest with a crest on the pocket, as well as a crisp white blouse. "Cute, huh?" I can tell by her expression, she's kidding.

"I used to think it would be cool to go to a private school with uniforms like this," I admit sadly.

"Well, you will be going to a private school . . ." She chuckles. "Of sorts."

I give her a dismal look as I begin getting dressed. I layer on the strange clothes and eventually she helps me with the navy blue tie. Then she explains about the few things she's packed in a handbag for me. I have a feeling I'm not going to remember to reapply my lip gloss.

When I'm completely together and she stands me in front of the mirror, I stare at the strange image. Who is this dark-haired girl in this conservative-looking outfit? Well, except that the skirt's pretty short. Other than that, I could be on my way to some expensive preppy school. It's all very surreal . . . and sickening.

"I see you're all done in here." Jimmy walks in without knocking, coming over to get a better look at me. He nods with approval. "Nice work, Desiree." He goes over to her, grabs her by the arm, slaps her across her face, then shoves her to her bed. "I'll deal with you later."

"Looks like you dealt with her already." I glare at him.

He raises his hand as if he's going to smack me, too.

"Go ahead," I say. "Blacken my eyes and bloody my nose and maybe Mr. T will demand a refund and send me back here."

"We don't want you back," he growls at me. "You're way too much trouble." He looks at his watch. "Well, you've got some time to kill until then." He grabs me by the arm, shoving the overnight bag at me. "Get moving." As we leave Desiree's room, he dead bolts her door and drops the keys into his pocket.

"You don't trust anyone, do you?" I try to sound glib, but I'm plotting. I glance at the bag in my hand—could I swing it hard enough to knock him over the head, make him fall down the stairs, grab his keys, and make a fast break?

But he doesn't give me the chance as he shoves me in front of him toward the stairs. "Move it!" He swears at me. "I will be so glad to see the last of you."

I want to tell him the feeling's mutual but control myself. And although I know I'm supposed to pray for my enemies, I can't do it with any sincerity at the moment. Maybe when I'm free of this place, because I still believe I'm getting out of here. I just don't know how.

I spot Ruby in the kitchen. And when she sees me, she hurries over. "Is she going to Mr. T now?"

"What's it to you?" Jimmy growls at her.

"I just want to say good-bye."

"Fine, why don't you come with us? You and Tatiana can both tell her good-bye together." He laughs as he pushes us back toward the bedroom that's been my jail cell these past couple of weeks. "I'll lock you all in together and maybe I can enjoy a little peace and quiet for a change." Ruby's eyes widen as he shoves her into the room with me. "Have fun, girls." He points at me. "Don't wrinkle that uniform!" Then he slams the door shut and the lock snaps into place.

"I'm sorry," I tell Ruby. "I didn't mean for you to get locked up too."

"It's okay." She makes a nervous smile.

"What's going on?" Tatiana asks sleepily, sitting up from where she was reclined on the bed. She grins to see my outfit. "Well, of course." Now she frowns. "Why is Ruby in here?"

"Everyone's in lockdown," I explain. "Except Kandy . . . the mole."

"Yeah, well, don't say we didn't warn you," Tatiana says. "So how is the great escape coming?"

Leaning against the wall, I scowl down at the floor, studying the weird blue pumps and the white knee-high socks . . . still wondering over Mr. T's taste in women's wear.

"I have something for you," Ruby whispers urgently.

"What?" I look at Ruby, watching as she removes what looks like a wadded tissue from the pocket of her cutoffs. With a mysterious smile, she hands it to me.

"What have you done?" Tatiana asks cautiously.

"Open it," Ruby tells me.

I slowly unfold the tissue to see about twenty or so small white pills. "Huh? What is it?"

"Sleeping pills," Ruby whispers. "At least I think they are."

"What for?" Tatiana comes over to inspect them.

"To knock out Mr. T," Ruby says.

Tatiana nods approvingly. "Good idea."

"How do I do it?"

"You should crush them," Tatiana advises me.

I look around the room and finally decide to use the heels of my pumps, grinding the white pills between them until I have a tiny pile of white dust.

"You need something that it can slide out of easily," Tatiana says. "Like an envelope." We look around the room and then Ruby gets the idea to tear a page from one of her books. We fold it into an envelope and shake the powder into it. Then I fold it closed and slip it into my vest pocket.

"No," Tatiana says. "A pocket is too obvious. The security guard might pat you down."

"Security guard?"

"Yeah. One of Mr. T's girls came back here for a couple days. She told me his house is this huge mansion with security and guard dogs and alarms and stuff."

"Really?"

"Yeah. She said it was kind of a fortress."

"I appreciate the head's up, but even if I knock Mr. T out, how will I get past all that?"

"What about all your faith?" Tatiana says in a slightly teasing way.

I nod. "Yeah. You're right. I'll just need to trust God."

"Your bra," Tatiana says to me.

"Huh?"

She points to the tiny envelope of crushed pills. "Put it in your bra. Even if they pat you down, they probably won't feel it in there."

I secure the envelope in the center of the bra and we all agree that's the best place. Then Tatiana starts coaching me for ways to get Mr. T to turn his back on me while I tamper with his drink. Between her and Ruby, we manage to create a script of sorts.

"How can I thank you?" I finally say, so encouraged by the

way these girls have turned around and started to trust me. It seems nothing short of miraculous.

"You can thank us by getting free," Tatiana tells me.

"And maybe you can help us get free," Ruby says.

I grab her hand. "I'll do everything I can." Then it hits me. "I need to know the address of this house."

Tatiana looks worried. "I don't know . . ."

"You don't know the address?" I question.

"No, if this house gets busted, we could end up—"

"If Serena gets free, we'll probably have to leave anyway," Ruby reasons. And then she tells me the address including the name of the town. I'm just repeating it over and over in my head when Jimmy shows up, announcing it's time for everyone to get ready for the "evening's activities."

He frowns at Ruby and Tatiana. "You girls need to go do something about those faces. Get Desiree to help you cover up your little bumps and bruises." The girls and I say a quick goodbye and then, like I'm a four-year-old, Jimmy warns once again not to mess up my uniform. "Your ride will be here in twenty minutes." Then he locks me up again.

I spend the remainder of my time pacing and praying and rehearsing the lines Tatiana and Ruby helped me with—as well as the address of this house. I'm so glad Ruby told me, and I want it fixed firmly in my memory.

And then—just like that—Jimmy and Kandy appear, and with his stun gun aimed threateningly, he waits as Kandy binds my hands together in front of me and blindfolds me. They roughly lead me through the house and we pass through what feels like the laundry room into the garage and finally into what feels like the backseat of what's probably an expensive vehicle— I can smell leather.

"Here's her bag." Jimmy tosses it at my feet.

"Even if Serena doesn't come back here, we'd like the bag back," Kandy says. "We girls can use those things."

"Yeah, well, we'll see about that," a man answers from in front of me. His voice sounds vaguely familiar, but I can't quite place it. "Buckle her up," he snaps. "I don't want her pulling any stunts on the way over there." Suddenly I remember the guy named Mitch who delivered the sweatshop workers the other day, and I'm sure he's the one in front.

Someone buckles me into the seat and the car door slams and now the vehicle begins to move. For a while no one speaks and I am using my full concentration to keep my composure. I do some deep breathing to calm myself and then I begin to silently pray.

"She's a pretty one," Mitch says in a sleazy tone.

"Yeah, she sure is," an equally sleazy voice says from the other side of the backseat. I feel a hand creeping up my thigh, and I let out a scream.

"Hey man, don't mess with the merchandise," Mitch warns. "You know what Mr. T says about that kind of stuff."

"Yeah, yeah . . ." His hand is gone now, but my skin is still crawling.

The two men laugh like this is funny, making smutty remarks back and forth. Meanwhile I'm trying to remember anything and everything about these guys, details I might be able to share with law enforcement. More than anything I'd like to see these guys arrested and put away. Then after what seems like at least twenty minutes, the car stops and I hear the window go down.

"Don't forget Tom said they changed the code," the guy beside me says.

"Yeah, yeah, I got it," Mitch responds, and after a few seconds the window goes back up. I'm guessing this is a gated area but don't know if it's a private home or a neighborhood. I'm praying it's not a private home. That would make escaping even more difficult.

We drive for a few more minutes as the man beside me talks to someone on his phone, announcing that we're almost there. And then after the car comes to a complete stop, my blindfold is removed. "Is that better?" the man beside me asks.

I blink into the light, then quickly take in his shaved head, dark glasses, and smirking grin. He appears to be in his thirties or forties and I notice a tattoo on his left hand. Some kind of symbol. I also notice the shining blade of a knife in his other hand.

"Now if you promise to be a good little girl, I'll cut your hands free before we go inside. Mr. T prefers it that way, but if you're going to be difficult, we'll just wait until you're inside."

"I won't be difficult." Not yet anyway.

"Smart girl." He slices through the cords with one quick stroke.

I rub my wrists and wait. As far as I can see, the car is parked under some kind of entry to a house that appears to be made of stone. The fortress. And now one of the huge wooden doors opens and a tall man dressed in black steps out, looking from side to side, and then he nods toward the car.

"Scotty's giving us the green light," Mitch says. "Take her out."

"Here's the deal," the man next to me says as he gives me a shove from behind. "Don't try anything and no one gets hurt. Just get out of the car and we'll walk over to Scotty nice and easy. You got that?"

"Yes."

He reaches in front of me and opens the door, pushing me out so we both emerge from the car almost simultaneously. "Here's your bag." He hands it to me. "Here's your girl," he says to Scotty.

Scotty just nods, and taking me by the arm, he escorts me up to the big double doors, but before we go inside, I glance to my right and am reassured to see that it looks like this house is part of a neighborhood—a very swanky neighborhood. But having houses nearby gives me hope.

Scotty leads me into a dimly lit foyer. "Welcome," he says in a deep voice.

"Thanks . . ." I mumble as the door closes.

"Right this way." He leads me toward a gracefully curving staircase. "Mr. T is up there." His grip on my arm tightens as he leads me up the stairs, almost as if he expects me to put up a fight. But I just go along with him. My plan is to play this calm and cool.

"This is a beautiful house," I say, trying to sound natural.

"Yes, it is." He pauses at the top of the stairs, looking directly at me. "And just so you know, it's a very secure house. We have a top-of-the-line security system." He points out a surveillance camera on a high wall. "Always watching." He walks me down a hallway with several doors. "And we have a pair of Dobermans that guard the grounds. So everyone stays very safe here." He smiles, and if I'd met him under other circumstances, I would've assumed he was just a nice guy. "I hope you enjoy your stay, miss."

"Thank you." I force a nervous smile.

"The master suite," he says as he taps lightly on the door. My knees begin to really shake as the door is opened.

"Come in, come in," a friendly male voice says. I feel like I'm about to faint or throw up or maybe even both. Instead I pray for deliverance.

CHAPTER 19

Scotty gives me a little boost into the room, and suddenly I am standing face-to-face with a man, but I'm surprised to see he is nothing like the monster I've imagined.

"Are you Mr. T?" I ask as the door behind me closes.

"That's what some people call me." He smiles as he smoothes his graying hair back. It's damp and I'm guessing he's just taken a shower. Now he reaches behind me, quickly punching a security code onto the security pad by the door. No keys needed here. Just numbers. I wish I'd been watching more closely. "And you are Serena Delray," he says in a friendly way. "It's a pleasure to meet you."

I bite my lip, trying to think of something to say, but everything feels so bizarre and unreal. Mr. T just looks like an ordinary man. Okay, a really wealthy ordinary man. But he's not even big. Probably just an inch or two taller than me. Average height and weight and rather average looking. He could be somebody's dad . . . or grandpa.

He puts a hand on my shoulder. "Are you all right?"

"Uh . . . well, not really," I say in a shaky voice. "I, uh, I feel kind of faint."

"Come over here and sit down." He gently leads me over to a

seating area by a large set of windows. "You're probably just having a bad case of nerves. It's to be expected." He eases me down into a brown velvet chair and I sink into its comforting form.

I study his face as he stands over me. It's tanned and lined, but it doesn't look unkind or criminal or menacing. And yet he does this? He pays big money to bring in girls like me? I cannot even wrap my head around it.

"I know what you're thinking." He sits in the velvet chair across from me. He studies me with cool blue eyes. "You don't understand why someone of my class and caliber pays to have girls brought to him, right?"

I nod, swallowing against the dryness in my throat. "It seems odd."

"Yes, I'm sure it does." He frowns.

Suddenly I remember the packet of crushed pills in my bra and I remember the lines I rehearsed earlier. I reach up and touch my throat. "I feel kind of parched. May I please have a drink?"

"Certainly." He stands. "What would you like?"

"Just water is fine. Or soda if you have it."

"Oh, I have everything." He goes over to what looks like a mini bar and opens a small fridge and lists off the options.

"Cola is fine."

I hear the sound of ice clinking into a glass and before long he joins me, not with just one glass, but two. Exactly like Tatiana had predicted. I quickly suck down my cola, as if I'm parched, which I actually am.

"Need a refill?"

Now I make an uncertain expression. "Yes . . . I suppose so." I point at his glass that has something clear with a lime. "What are you drinking?"

He chuckles. "Gin and tonic."

"Is that alcohol?"

He holds it up, takes a sip, then nods. "You bet it is."

"I've never really drank alcohol. But maybe it's time I gave it a try. I mean, if it's okay."

"Sure. I'll make you one."

Then as he returns to the bar, I discreetly slip the packet from my bra. Hopefully I'm not on camera in here. As he mixes my drink, I open the packet and slip it into the sleeve of my left hand. And just like Tatiana predicted, he returns quickly with my drink, setting it down on the table between the two chairs.

"Thank you," I say as I reach for it and take a big sip, which tastes so nasty I don't even have to pretend to hate it. I gasp and sputter and make a face. "Ugh. I'm sorry, but that tastes terrible. How can you stand it?"

He just laughs. "I suppose it is an acquired taste."

I wrinkle my nose. "Not for me." Now I get a thoughtful look. "But aren't there drinks that are sweet and fruity? A friend of mine likes something called Long Island iced tea. Do you think that would be good?"

His brows arch slightly. "Yes. That might be just what you need to help you relax a little." He takes my previous drink and returns to the bar, and as he's distracted by pulling out some bottles and ingredients, I slip out the packet and quickly dump it into his drink, praying that I'm not being watched right now. To my dismay the powder is sitting on the surface of the drink, just like Ruby predicted.

"This is a really pretty house," I say to him, keeping my eye on him as I attempt to mix the powder into his drink with my finger. "You must be a very wealthy man." I lean back just as he looks up.

"Oh yes, you could say that."

I stand up now, acting interested in the view from the window but really looking for my next opportunity to stir the powder down into that drink. "That's a beautiful backyard. And a swimming pool, too. Wow." Seeing him focused on opening a bottle, I reach over and continue stirring frantically, keeping my eyes on him the whole while.

"Come on over here," he calls out.

Worried that he's suspicious, I go on over.

He watches as I walk toward him. "Very pretty." He nods with approval as he stirs a tall glass. "Tom tells me you're from Los Angeles."

I nod nervously. "That's right."

"Well, that should do it." He hands me the drink.

I take a cautious sniff.

"Go ahead, try it."

I put my hand to my head. "Mind if I sit back down first? I'm still feeling a little dizzy."

"By all means." He waves his hand toward the chairs. "Sit. I always like to get to know my dates. Makes it more personal, if you know what I mean."

I shrug as I go back to my chair. "I guess. But to be honest, this is all completely new to me."

He smiles as he sits down. "Yes, that is precisely how I like it, my dear."

I hold up my drink. "Well, what do you say? I mean, is there a toast? Or is it just bottoms up?"

He chuckles as he picks up his glass, holding it toward me. I try not to look at his drink, but I'm praying there's no telltale powder floating on top and that there's no bad taste, although I'm not sure how anything could taste worse than the gin and tonic as it was. "Here's to you, my dear girl, and to a memorable evening. You just let Mr. T take care of you and all will be well. I promise."

We clink glasses and then I take a swig. "Hey, that's not too bad. Is that really a Long Island iced tea?"

"As best I can recall, it is." He takes a sip of his drink, and I realize it's up to me to distract him with chatter, to keep him talking and drinking until it's gone. Every last drop.

"This is an interesting outfit you picked out for me," I say as I smooth out my skirt. "Is there any special reason?"

He nods with a faraway look. "Yes, I suppose there is."

When he doesn't expound on his answer, I decide to run with it anyway. "Did you go to an expensive private school as a boy?"

He smiles. "As a matter of fact."

"And I'll bet you had a girlfriend there, right?"

He just takes another sip, as if he doesn't want to really talk about this.

"Or maybe it was a crush?" I take a sip. "There was a girl you really wanted to get to know, but maybe you were shy . . . or she was shy . . . but I'll bet she was really pretty." I force a smile. "And I'm sure you were good-looking too."

His brows barely lift and I can tell that I'm making him slightly uncomfortable, but at least he's still drinking. I continue talking to him, spinning a story about how I had a crush on a boy, but the boy didn't know I existed. Part of it's true and part of it's make-believe. "But then I started to get pretty. And Leo started paying attention to me." I lean forward, peering at Mr. T. "He wanted to go out with me. And you know what I did?"

"No, what did you do?"

"I told him to forget about it," I say triumphantly.

Mr. T laughs. "Good for you."

"Yes." I hold my glass up like I'm making another toast. "Here's to holding out for you." I feel like hurling at this thought, but I am determined to get that drink down him.

He takes another drink. "You're quite a girl, Serena."

"Thank you." Now I look at my glass and am surprised to see it's only half full. Hopefully it's not enough to really make me drunk. That would not be good.

"Go ahead and finish it," he urges me. "I think it's helping you to relax."

I giggle and point to his drink. "Is that helping you relax?"

He chuckles like this is funny, and then to my relief, he downs the last of his drink. And now I pretend to be sipping on mine, but I'm really worried that I'm starting to feel light-headed. So I stand. "Hey, do you have anything to eat up here?" I walk back over to the bar area.

"Oh yeah, sure. There's cheese and olives in the fridge. Maybe some fruit, too. And some crackers in that cabinet. I've arranged for us to have a late dinner . . . after we get to know each other better."

I continue chattering at him as I help myself to his food, and I can tell by his slowing responses that the pills are starting to take effect. But not wanting him to be suspicious, I keep talking and even go back to the chairs, offering a piece of cheese to him. But he just waves his hand. However, he is slumping in the chair now.

I keep on talking, just the way Ruby told me the girl in the book did, only I speak a little slower. Maybe I hope to hypnotize him as I ramble on and on, telling him of how I once dreamed of being a model and how my elderly neighbor was helping me, how she used to be a professional model but manages a clothing

store now. "She thought I might have what it takes." I walk back
and forth, showing him some of the moves she taught me.

"But then Mrs. Norbert fell and broke her hip," I continue
slowly, noticing that his eyes are closed. "It was pretty sad. She
had to go live with her daughter and . . ." I pause to see if he's
even listening, but he appears to be soundly sleeping.

Suddenly I'm worried that I could be watched, but I don't
want to blow it by looking around for a security camera. Instead
I pretend like he's still awake. "Now, Mr. T, if you'll excuse me,
I need to use the restroom." I put down my half-full glass. Then
I go off in search of a bathroom, hoping there might be a way to
sneak out a window. But even though I can get it open, when
I peer down I see that it's a straight drop down to the front
circular driveway. Even if I could scale the stone siding, it would
be dangerous and I suspect a surveillance camera might be out
there.

I flush the toilet for effect, then wander back out to check
on my host. He seems to be completely knocked out. I actually
wonder if I've given him a dose big enough to kill him. I hope
not. I'd rather he go to prison than die.

I look out the window that overlooks the pool, but seeing
the dogs down there like Scotty told me, I know that's not a
good idea. Next I explore behind a door and find a big closet
with built-in drawers and dozens of men's suits and shirts and
things. But no windows, and as far as I can see, there is no way
out of here. I go look in another closet that, to my surprise,
seems to belong to a woman. Does Mr. T have a wife? And if so,
where is she? And what does she think about his secret life? Does
she even know?

Like the other closet, I assume this one has no window, but
then I notice something up near the ceiling behind some hat

boxes. I pull out some of the built-in drawers, and using them like stairs, I climb up until I can see that it is indeed a window — a long, narrow one, but it does open. By now I'm pretty sure that if there are surveillance cameras in the master suite, they must be turned off. Maybe for Mr. T's privacy. But even if they're not, I'm going to try to make my break.

Praying that I'm thin enough to fit through the narrow opening, I squeeze my head out and look down. Thankfully, this window is not facing the front street or the backyard. It seems to be on the side of the house and about six feet below is a section of tiled roof. I go out the window backward, easing myself down feet first onto what look like slippery tiles.

With a prayer, I begin my descent, sliding out the window until I'm holding to the edge of it and getting my feet securely on the tiles. Now I crouch down, looking around to see if there's a camera nearby or if anyone down below can see me.

Satisfied that I'm still in the clear, I work my way to the side of this overhang, the end that's toward the street since I want to avoid those dogs. When I get to the edge, I can't believe my luck. Directly below is some kind of garden structure with flowering vines growing over it. I'm not sure if it's strong enough to support my weight, but it's a chance I must take. I ease myself onto it and it seems to be holding. Feeling like a monkey, I work my way out to the street side and then swing down, landing in the grass.

I don't pause to think, I just take off running. My plan is to get several houses away from here. As I run, I pray that God will show me which house to stop at. I start to head up to a big brick house with an American flag flying out front, but something stops me. I have nothing against flags. But something just doesn't feel right.

So, trying not to look too conspicuous, I turn and continue on down the street, pausing by a tall white house with a pair of pink flamingos in the front yard. These plastic birds look out of place in this fancy, upscale neighborhood. And yet they're inviting. Hoping these people have a sense of humor as well as good hearts, I run up to the door and ring the doorbell.

CHAPTER 20

Cowering in the shadows of the covered porch area, I glance up and down the street to see if anyone is watching or coming after me. Everything looks perfectly normal, and yet my heart is pounding in my chest like a bass drum. *Please be home,* I pray silently, *please be home!*

An older woman opens the door, peering curiously at me. "Yes?"

"Sorry to disturb you, ma'am," I say breathlessly. "But I need your help. I've been kidnapped and—"

"Are you serious?" She frowns doubtfully at me, peering over my shoulder. "Is this some kind of joke? Candid camera?"

"No joke," I say quickly. "I swear to you—as God is my witness, *it's true.* My name is Simi Fremont. I was abducted from the LA area a couple weeks ago. My mom's name is Ginnie Fremont and—" I start to cry. "Please—*please*—help me before the men come after me again."

Just like that, she grabs me by the arm, jerks me into her house, and locks the door behind me. "You better be on the up-and-up," she says sternly. But now I'm bawling uncontrollably. It's like all the emotions I've been holding inside me are bursting out and I can't stop myself.

The woman goes for her phone. "I'm calling 911 right now," she says like it's a warning. "So if this is a stunt, you'd better — "

"No, please, don't call 911. They'll send out the police and I've heard you can't trust them — some of the police are involved in human trafficking and they'll just send me — "

"Human trafficking?" Her eyes grow wide.

"Yes. And one of your neighbors is involved." I point down the street. "I don't know his name. He goes by Mr. T and he's connected to the traffickers. They take girls to him. I just escaped his house. Please, please, just let me call my mom. *Please!"*

"What's her number?"

I tell her Mom's cell number. And just like that this woman is dialing and then talking to my mom. "Hello, I'm Mrs. Moller," she begins calmly. I listen with pounding heart and disbelief as she explains what I just told her. "Really?" She looks genuinely surprised. "So it's true that she was abducted?" She listens with a horrified look, then hands the phone to me. "Oh my goodness. I'm so sorry."

"Mom!" I sob into the phone.

"Simi! Is it really you?"

"Yes. I'm in Oregon. Somewhere near Portland, I think."

"Are you okay?"

"Yes. But I'm still in danger. And you need to get help for me."

"Did you call 911? Do you want me to — ?"

"No. That will get the police — and some of them are crooked. It's a human-trafficking group that kidnapped me. They're a huge organization, Mom. You need the FBI or — "

"Yes. We've been speaking to some FBI agents."

"We?"

"Michelle and Trista and I have all been working together. Everyone in the church has been praying. Now tell me where you are, Simi. What's the address?"

I look at Mrs. Moller, who has flopped down into a chair. She's fanning her face with a magazine as if she's in shock. "Can you tell my mom where I'm at?" I hold the phone to her.

She takes the phone and gives Mom the information. Then she hands it back to me.

"Are you okay?" I ask Mrs. Moller.

She waves her hand. "Don't worry. I'll be fine."

"I don't know what to do," I say to Mom. "I'm so afraid. What if they come down here and find me?"

"Just stay on the phone," she says. "Trista is here with me. Right now she's calling the FBI on her cell phone. Agent Barclay's been helping us." I can hear Mom talking to Trista, and within seconds we are having a three-way conversation with my mom talking to both me and the FBI agent at the same time. He asks questions and we're all exchanging information back and forth.

"And I want to give you the address of the house where I was held captive," I say urgently. "I told them I'd send help."

"Yes," Barclay says eagerly. "We can really use that."

I tell him the name of the town and address as well as some description of the house and the locks and the girls who are kept there. "But they'll be out tonight. I don't know what time they'll get back."

He assures me they'll do surveillance.

"And some of the girls want help. But they feel trapped and scared." I tell him their real names—the ones I know—and where they came from.

"This is excellent," he tells me. "Very useful."

"I have more names too. And. Oh yeah, I nearly forgot—

there are twenty-three women and children being held captive in the basement. And they looked half starved. I gave them what food I could find, but they must be very hungry."

He assures me they will be rescued, and Mrs. Moller puts a hand to her forehead and gasps.

"Where are you now?" the agent asks. "I mean, inside the house?"

I look around. "I guess it's the living room."

"Can you get into a safer room? A room with a lock where you can wait until our agents get there?"

I quickly relay this to Mrs. Moller, and she leads me up to a master bedroom where she locks the door. Then to be even safer, we go into the bathroom and she locks that door as well. For the first time in days, I'm thankful for locks. I explain to the agent where we're hiding and he continues to ask questions about the location of Mr. T's house. I describe it to him, saying it's about four houses down from Mrs. Moller's.

"Is it on the same side of the street?"

"Yes." But when he asks north or south, I don't know.

"Let me speak to him," Mrs. Moller says suddenly. "I know the house Simi just described. It's north of my house—five houses down. I don't know the couple personally, but their name is Thompkins. Also you should know that this is a gated neighborhood. You need the pass numbers to get in." Then she gives him the code as well as more specific directions to her street. "Yes, I'll put Simi back on." She hands the phone back to me.

"When will help get here?" I ask anxiously.

"The team's been dispatched, Simi. But it's going to take about ten minutes. We want them to be very discreet. Agent Anderson will come to the door. She's a tall blonde woman in

her thirties. We want to get you and Mrs. Moller out first—
before we deal with Mr. Thompkins."

"Oh, yeah . . ." I say slowly. "That reminds me."

"What?"

"I—uh—well . . . to escape I kind of drugged him."

"Drugged him?"

"One of the girls at the house gave me sleeping pills to put
in his drink. I crushed them and put them in his gin and tonic.
And he fell asleep."

"What kind of pills? Over the counter? Prescription?
Barbiturates?"

"I don't know. Ruby called them sleeping pills, but the girl
she stole them from is a serious drug user."

"Which girl?"

"Kandy Kane. I don't know her real name." I describe her as
well as the pills. "And there were about twenty I think." Now
I'm worried. "What if I killed him?"

"We'll dispatch an ambulance for Mr. Thompkins."

"Oh . . . okay."

"Don't worry about it, Simi," Mom jumps in now. "You were
just doing what you needed to do to get away from them. Even
if he dies, it's not your fault. Do not blame yourself."

We talk awhile longer, I answer more of the agent's questions, and Mom occasionally says something, and finally after
what seems like hours, he tells me that the FBI car is pulling up
to the house. "It's a gray SUV," he says, and I relay this to Mrs.
Moller and we go out into the bedroom and look out a window
that overlooks the street. "I see it. It's pulling up in front."
I watch eagerly. "A blonde woman is getting out."

There's a long pause and Agent Barclay tells me that Agent
Anderson has given the all clear. "Go with her," he tells me.

"You and Mrs. Moller act as if you're simply going out with a friend."

We do as we're told, and within minutes we're being whisked away. Tears of relief are pouring down my face and Mrs. Moller hugs me tightly. "You were so brave, dear. I'm very proud of you."

"Thank you for letting me into your home. I don't know what I would've done without you." Now I explain how I was praying for the right house.

She squeezes my hand. "I'm glad God led you to me."

"It was the pink flamingos that made me knock on your door."

She laughs. "My sister put those there for my sixty-fifth birthday last week. It was a joke, but I decided to leave them there a bit. Just to aggravate the neighbors."

I call my mom, reassuring her that I'm okay. And Mrs. Moller calls her sister and before long they are dropping her off at her sister's house, where she will spend the night. Agent Anderson promises to keep her informed about when it's safe to return to her home. We hug and I thank her again.

"I can't wait to tell Dorothy about my exciting adventure," Mrs. Moller says as she gets out, hurrying to meet the gray-haired woman coming out to the car.

As the car continues, I lean back and sigh. "God answered my prayers," I say quietly. "I knew he would."

Agent Anderson nods. "You're a very lucky girl, Simi." Then as we drive into the city, where she insists I must be examined at the hospital, she continues to ask me questions. I tell her about Marcia and Bryce and Rod, and it sounds like the FBI is already looking for them. I tell her about everyone and everything I can remember, almost like I'm emptying my brain. But she is grateful and appears to be getting it all down.

"I'm worried about Mom and Trista and Michelle." I explain the threats that Marcia and Bryce made, how they would go after my family and friends if I messed up. "How soon will it be until they know what I did?"

"Hard to say. But I'll let Agent Barclay know that we might need a relocation plan. Do you think you'll want to testify in court against these people?" She studies me carefully.

"Absolutely. I'll do everything possible to get them all behind bars."

"Good girl." She pats my shoulder. "So many times the girls are so intimidated and scared—they refuse to help."

"Should I be scared?"

"We'll do everything we can to protect you. Most of all, we'll try to get these creeps off the streets. That's the best way to protect you."

It's after nine by the time we get to the hospital, where to my relief, I'm given a meal—and I've never been so thankful to see fresh vegetables before. I also get a thorough exam and I'm not surprised to see that I've lost twelve pounds. Photos are taken and I assure the doctor and Agent Anderson that despite being deprived of food and water at times, as well as the general nasty conditions of the place, I feel perfectly fine. Even so, Agent Anderson insists that I need to remain in the hospital overnight.

"Both for your safety and for our convenience since it's late. But don't worry, there'll be a guard by your door."

"Is that really necessary?"

"Hopefully not. But you're a valuable witness for us."

Now I remember Mr. T (aka Mr. Thompkins) and I ask her if there's any chance he could wind up in this same hospital as me.

"No chance whatsoever," she assures me. "He's at St. Vincent's."

"Oh . . . is he okay?"

"It sounds like he's going to make it."

It's strange to feel relieved that such an evil man isn't dead, but I do. I'd rather he went to prison than the cemetery. "When can I go home?"

"Maybe tomorrow or the next day. And we'll probably have to go by car. It's possible that they'll be watching for you at PDX by the time we could get a flight." Then she offers to spend the night at the hospital with me. But the nurses have been so nice and friendly and the guard by the door looks dependable, so I assure her that I'll be all right.

"God is taking care of me," I tell her as I finish off a chocolate sundae the nurse just brought me for dessert.

Agent Anderson just smiles and nods. "I believe he is."

After she leaves, I use the cell phone she left with me to call Mom and then Michelle. It feels so good to talk to both of them, and I can't wait to go home. But at the same time, I am so sleepy and I know tomorrow will be busy. It feels amazing to be clean and wearing a clean gown—and even more amazing to be in a real bed with clean, fresh-smelling bedding. I don't think I'll ever take such ordinary things for granted again.

But before I go to sleep, I thank God for delivering me and I pray for everyone back at the house. I can't even begin to imagine what will transpire tonight, but I beg God to watch out for Tatiana and Ruby and Desiree, as well as the twenty-three captives in the basement. I even pray for Jimmy and Kandy, because I know they're in danger too.

CHAPTER 21

The next day, Agent Anderson brings me fresh clothes, and before long we're being transported via car to California. As the car moves down I-5, she continues to question me, trying to fill in as many gaps as possible. And now she has photos on her laptop, mug shots for me to peruse in the hopes we'll get a firm identity on some of the low-life traffickers. As we travel, she gets reports on how things are progressing in Portland.

"We had to move fast last night," she tells me as she sets her phone down. "But it's paid off."

"Are the girls okay? And the people in the basement?"

"The house was surrounded at around five this morning. It took a few hours, since they weren't sure how many firearms were involved, but everyone in the house was eventually taken into custody without incident."

I am so thankful that tears fill my eyes. "And what will happen to them?"

"After they're questioned and examined, they'll be placed in a safe house. If they're underage, their parents or guardians will be contacted."

"Can I have contact with any of them?"

"Do you want to?" She frowns like this might not be a good idea.

"Yes. I know some of the girls have rough situations at home. I don't want them to end up in the same situation again. And I think our church might be willing to help out. If they need it."

"Okay. I'll make sure that they know this. But for your protection they will have to contact you through us." She lets me send them messages through the agent who's helping them up in Portland.

It's after dark by the time we make it into the LA area, but to my surprise, the car sails right past the exit to my town and a familiar chill runs through me as I remember how Rod took a different route on the way to my "interview" with Marcia and Bryce. I look questionably at Agent Anderson now. Surely she's not a human trafficker. "Uh . . . where are we going?"

She looks up from her laptop. "Oh, didn't I tell you that you and your mom are being relocated?"

I let out a sigh, and before long we're pulling into a subdivision where all the houses look almost exactly alike. "Wow. It would be easy to get lost in here."

"Exactly." She nods. "Sameness equals anonymity." The car winds around the streets and eventually pulls into the driveway of a tan split-level house. "Here we are."

She escorts me directly into the house where Mom and Trista and even the twins happily greet me. After we hug and laugh and dance and rejoice, Mom explains that she couldn't leave Trista and the kids behind at the apartments. I pick up Lacy and peer into her face. "We're like one big happy family now," I gladly tell her.

"There's safety in numbers," Agent Anderson tells me. "But just to be really safe, I want everyone to keep a low profile for the next few weeks. Just until everything shakes down." She hands Mom a folder. "I'm sure Agent Barclay has explained all this, but there are some good hints and suggestions in this packet. And, of course, we'll be in regular contact. Even more so as the trials draw near."

. . . .

By September, we're all still living in the split-level, and I'm back in school. But not my old school, and thanks to the FBI, I go by a different name. Marcia and Bryce and Rod, as well as several others in the LA area, have been arrested and charged and are being held on huge amounts of bail. And more arrests are anticipated. Even more arrests have been made in the Portland area. It's only one drop in the big bucket of human trafficking, but to those who've been rescued or even spared from abduction, it is an important drop.

Because we've been somewhat confined to the house, I've spent a fair amount of time researching human trafficking and have been surprised at how widespread and growing this heinous crime is. But just hearing numbers isn't nearly as startling as imagining the faces behind these numbers. Having known Tatiana, Ruby, Desiree, and the others makes it much more real. So much so that I have decided to do something about it. I plan to go to college in pursuit of a degree that will lead me into a career to help prevent human trafficking. I'm not sure if it will be the FBI, like Agent Anderson, or something else. But I feel certain that God is calling me in this direction.

Also, after I've testified at the various trials along the West Coast, and after the criminals are safely locked up for a long, long time, I plan to start speaking to kids my age about human trafficking. I don't want to just stand up there and rattle off numbers though — even if this is a multibillion-dollar business with more than 2.5 million forced into slavery around the globe.

Sure, those are big numbers, but they are impersonal. I want people to understand that the teens in the slave trade are real people — just regular kids like you and me. More than that, I want to warn them about how this can happen — in a heartbeat — to anyone. Not so that teens will be afraid and looking over their shoulders all the time, but so they will be smart . . . and not fall for stupid lies.

Thanks to Agent Anderson, I recently reconnected to Tatiana by e-mail. She could hardly believe that I actually made it out of Mr. T's house and delivered on my promise to send help to them. Well, some of them thought it was help. Apparently Jimmy was not terribly happy — and even less happy when he was arrested.

After the house was raided, all the girls were taken to a safe house. But according to Tatiana, Kandy ran away the very next day and Tatiana suspects she's back at one of Tom's places. But Desiree moved into a group home, and Ruby is trying life with a foster family. Tatiana, to my surprise, has returned home — and even more surprising, she just started going to a church that meets in a coffeehouse. She's promised to stay in touch with me, and I have promised to continue praying for her. Isn't God amazing!

I learned a lot last summer. One of the most important things I learned is that God made us with the sensibility to discern dangerous situations so we can avoid falling into such dire circumstances. But sometimes we forget to listen to his voice . . . or we ignore his quiet warnings. The good news is that God isn't like us. He is always listening to us . . . he always hears us when we call.

···DISCUSSION QUESTIONS···

1. Simi had dreams of becoming rich and famous. Do you think this was a mistake? Why or why not?
2. Simi believed that God watches out for widows and orphans. Why do you think it went so wrong with her?
3. Simi's best friend, Michelle, was a "natural skeptic." Why do you think she was like that? Explain why you think that was good or bad.
4. Do you think Simi intentionally deceived her mother about interviewing with Top Models and Actors Inc.? And if so, why?
5. What was your first impression of Tatiana? Were you right or wrong about her?
6. Before reading this book, were you aware of human trafficking in this country? Did this book change your opinions or concerns at all? If so, how?
7. If you'd been in Simi's position (held against your will), would you have done anything differently? Describe what you would have done.
8. What did you think when Simi attempted to integrate herself with her captors? Did you see this as a compromise or clever? Explain.

9. What kind of people do you think are most at risk for being the victims of human trafficking? Do you know anyone like that? If so, what would you tell him or her?

10. Did you find it odd that Simi was willing to testify against the people who'd kidnapped and "trafficked" her? Why or why not?

11. Were you surprised that Kandy returned to her old ways? Explain.

12. After reading this story, do you feel more concerned about human trafficking in this country and the planet in general? If so, what would you do to change things?

The Headline Facts

• An estimated **2.5 million people** are in forced labor (including sexual exploitation) at any given time as a result of trafficking.[1] Of these:

   ▪ **1.4 million** — 56% are in Asia and the Pacific.
   ▪ **250,000** — 10% are in Latin America and the Caribbean.
   ▪ **230,000** — 9.2% are in the Middle East and Northern Africa.
   ▪ **130,000** — 5.2% are in sub-Saharan countries.
   ▪ **270,000** — 10.8% are in industrialized countries.
   ▪ **200,000** — 8% are in countries in transition.[2]

• **161 countries** are reported to be affected by human trafficking by being a source, transit, or destination count.[3]

---

1 International Labour Organization, *Forced Labour Statistics Factsheet* (2007).
2 International Labour Organization, *Forced Labour Statistics Factsheet* (2007).
3 United Nations Office on Drugs and Crime, *Trafficking in Persons: Global Patterns* (Vienna, 2006).

- People are reported to be trafficked from **127 countries** to be exploited in **137 countries**, affecting every continent and every type of economy.[4]

The Victims

- Most trafficking victims are **between 18 and 24 years old.**[5]
- An estimated **1.2 million children** are trafficked each year.[6]
- **95% of victims experience physical or sexual violence** during trafficking (based on data from selected European countries).[7]
- 43% of victims are used for **forced commercial sexual exploitation**, of whom 98% are women and girls.[8]
- 32% of victims are used for **forced economic exploitation**, of whom 56% are women and girls.[9]
- Many trafficking victims have at least a **middle-level education.**[10]

---

4 United Nations Office on Drugs and Crime, *Trafficking in Persons: Global Patterns* (Vienna, 2006).
5 International Organization for Migration, *Counter-Trafficking Database, 78 Countries, 1999-2006* (1999).
6 UNICEF, *UK Child Trafficking Information Sheet* (January 2003).
7 The London School of Hygiene & Tropical Medicine, *Stolen Smiles: a summary report on the physical and psychological health consequences of women and adolescents trafficked in Europe* (London, 2006).
8 International Labour Organization, *Forced Labour Statistics Factsheet* (2007).
9 International Labour Organization, *Forced Labour Statistics Factsheet* (2007).
10 International Organization for Migration, *Counter-Trafficking Database, 78 Countries, 1999-2006* (1999).

The Traffickers

- 52% of those recruiting victims are men, 42% are women, and 6% are both men and women.[11]
- In 54% of cases, the recruiter was a stranger to the victim; in 46% of cases, the recruiter was known to the victim.[12]
- Most suspects involved in the trafficking process are nationals of the country where the trafficking process is occurring.[13]

The Profits

- The estimated global annual profit made from the exploitation of all trafficked forced labor is **US$ 31.6 billion.**[14] Of this:

  - **US$ 15.5 billion** — 49% is generated in industrialized economies.
  - **US$ 9.7 billion** — 30.6% is generated in Asia and the Pacific.
  - **US$ 1.6 billion** — 5% is generated in sub-Saharan Africa.
  - **US$ 1.5 billion** — 4.7% is generated in the Middle East and North Africa.[15]
  - **US$ 1.3 billion** — 4.1% is generated in Latin America and the Caribbean.

---

11 International Organization for Migration, *Counter-Trafficking Database, 78 Countries, 1999-2006* (1999).

12 International Organization for Migration, *Counter-Trafficking Database, 78 Countries, 1999-2006* (1999).

13 United Nations Office on Drugs and Crime, *Trafficking in Persons: Global Patterns* (Vienna, 2006).

14 Patrick Besler, *Forced Labour and Human Trafficking: Estimating the Profits*, working paper (Geneva, International Labour Office, 2005).

15 Patrick Besler, *Forced Labour and Human Trafficking: Estimating the Profits*, working paper (Geneva, International Labour Office, 2005).

Prosecutions

- In 2006, there were only **5,808 prosecutions** and **3,160 convictions** throughout the world.[16]
- This means that for every 800 people trafficked, only one person was convicted in 2006.[17]

---

16 U.S. State Department, *Trafficking in Persons Report* (2007), 36.
17 U.S. State Department, *Trafficking in Persons Report* (2007), 36.

· · · · · ·ABOUT THE AUTHOR· · · · · ·

MELODY CARLSON has written more than two hundred books for all age groups, but she particularly enjoys writing for teens. Perhaps this is because her own teen years remain so vivid in her memory. After claiming to be an atheist at the ripe old age of twelve, she later surrendered her heart to Jesus and has been following him ever since. Her hope and prayer for all her readers is that each one would be touched by God in a special way through her stories. For more information, please visit Melody's website at www.melodycarlson.com.